GARY PAULSEN

Harris and Me

A Summer Remembered

A Yearling Book

Published by
Bantam Doubleday Dell Books for Young Readers
a division of
Bantam Doubleday Dell Publishing Group, Inc.
1540 Broadway
New York, New York 10036

ISBN: 0-440-40994-2

Reprinted by arrangement with Harcourt Brace & Company
Printed in the United States of America

May 1995

10 9 8 7 6 5 4 3 2 1

1

In which I meet Harris and am
exposed for the first time
to the vagaries of inflation

Meeting Harris would never have happened were it not for liberal quantities of Schlitz and Four Roses. For nearly all of my remembered childhood there was an open bottle of Schlitz on a table. My parents drank Four Roses professionally from jelly jars—neat, without diluting ice, water, or mix.

They were, consequently, vegetables most of the time—although the term vegetable connotes a feeling of calm that did not exist. They went through three phases of drunkenness: buzzed (happy), drunk (mean as snakes), and finally, obliterated (Four Roses coma).

Unfortunately the buzzed, or happy, stage only

lasted a short time, and it grew shorter as time progressed until they were pretty much mean whenever they were conscious.

Home became, finally, something of an impossibility for me and I would go to stay with relatives for extended periods of time.

By the time I was eleven I had stayed with several uncles, my grandmother, and an old Norwegian bachelor farmer who thought God lived in the haymow of his barn, where he was afraid to go without wearing a feed sack over his head. He told me God couldn't see through feed sacks and if God couldn't see you, you never died.

I had many uncles and shirttail relatives and when I was eleven a kind of rotation dumped me with Harris and his family.

The sheriff sent a deputy to pick me up and we left for the Larsons' place in late afternoon. They lived on a farm forty miles north of the town I lived in, yet it might as well have been on a different planet. The ride took about an hour and a half but it went through such varied terrain that before we had gone five miles I was in despair. For two or three of those miles the car moved past farm country that still seemed rather settled. Frequently there were tractors working in the fields and people who waved cheerfully, walking down the sides of the road. But soon the trees closed in, closer and thicker until they were a wall on either side and the road and car were enveloped in a curtain of green darkness. And there were no more open fields or driveways, just dirt tracks that disappeared into the forest and brush. It was like going off the edge of the earth on those old maps used by early explorers, into places where it said: There Be Monsters Here.

The deputy I was with spit constantly out the side window while extolling the virtues of the car— a 1949 Ford.

"It's got the V-eight," he told me. "Gets you a lot of power, the V-eight." *Spit.* "You need power for catching criminals while in hot pursuit." *Spit.*

"You want to be able to *move* this thing when you go into a hot pursuit situation." *Spit.*

There was absolutely no break in the forest. Black-green, densely vegetated, the summer northern woods fought right to the shoulder of the asphalt. Indeed, in places the trees came out over the road and made a green tunnel. I kept looking for an indication of life.

"People live here?" I asked finally.

"Sure." *Spit.* "Must be two, three hundred of 'em scattered around. You know, back in a ways."

The road grew more narrow, closed in until it nearly disappeared ahead of the car, and just when it seemed the car would have to dive into the trees, the deputy hung a left and the car bounced as we turned onto a dirt road—or, more accurately, a set of ruts.

We drove on this track for some miles—probably seven or eight—and again, just as the car seemed to run out of road, the deputy turned left once more. The tracks were still more narrow and I thought we would surely get stuck in the ruts, but suddenly we exploded out into a large area of cleared land.

"The Larson place," the deputy said.

The cleared land must have been more than half a square mile. It was planted in corn and small grain and looked rich and even. Along one side of the rectangular field lay a half-mile-long driveway, straight along the edge, and we now turned down it.

By this time I was nervous and had trouble sitting still. I had met the Larsons only once, though they were in some distant way related to me, and that had been four years earlier, when I was just seven. I had lived considerably since then—including almost three years in the Philippines where my father had been stationed—and I had almost no memory of how they looked, what they were like. There were four of them, I knew that: Knute, some kind of second uncle; his wife and my second aunt by marriage, Clair; their daughter, Glennis, who was fourteen; and my second cousin, Harris, who was nine.

I thought of what to do as we moved down the

drive. I had done this many times—been put in new places—and I had devised a method that worked. I pretended to be shy. Actually it was only partly pretending since I had a caution of meeting new people that often translated as flight. But shyness had served me well, and as we approached the house and farm buildings I began to withdraw.

They must have been expecting us because as the deputy worked the Ford down the driveway and we bounced into the yard, they were all standing there, waiting, one next to the other, where the driveway turned and widened next to the house.

The deputy lifted his weight out of the car— holding on to the top of the car door and grunting— and motioned for me to get out the other side.

I held back—the shyness kicking in—but in a moment realized that I would appear ridiculous if I stayed in the car and so got out but stood by the door waiting.

"Well, here he is," the deputy said. "I think we might be a bit early . . ."

His voice was fishing, ending in half a question, which didn't make any sense until my aunt Clair smiled, wiping her hands on her apron—an act I found later she did when worrying or thinking—and said, "Don't worry, Orlo. I made rhubarb pie and it's done. You aren't that early."

The deputy smiled, nodded, and turned back to

me and the car. "Don't hold back that way. Fetch your box and come on."

I still didn't move but Glennis, Harris's sister, who was coltish and smiled with her whole face, came forward and took my box out of the backseat of the car and started for the house with it. It was meant in a helpful way but posed a problem because I had my private stuff in the box. Even that wouldn't have been bad except that part of my private stuff was a collection of "art" photographs that I had bought for seventy centavos in the Philippines from a man on the street in Manila.

In higher circles the pictures would be known as artistic anatomical studies but the man who sold them to me called them "dourty peectures," which seemed far more accurate.

I enjoyed looking at them—being a student of art and at an age when the hormones seemed to dominate my every waking moment—but was fairly certain neither Glennis nor her mother would approve of them. This nervousness was compounded by the fact that the deputy was still there and I had somehow picked up the idea that the pictures were illegal. A mental image of me being arrested in front of all of them for possessing "dourty peectures" overcame my shyness, and I jumped forward and grabbed the box from Glennis.

All this time Harris had been standing, watching,

his hands behind him. I hadn't really looked at him, but when I moved to take the box from Glennis the grown-ups fell in together and started walking toward the house and Harris came up alongside me just as I grabbed the box.

Physically he was of a set piece with Glennis. Blond—hair bleached white by sun—face perpetually sunburned and red with a peeling nose, freckles sprinkled like brown pepper over everything, and even, white teeth, except that when Harris smiled there were two gone from the front. He was wearing a set of patched bib overalls. No shirt, no shoes—just freckles and the bibs, which were so large he seemed to move inside them.

"Hi."

He walked beside me, his hands still to his rear. I would subsequently find that this posture could be dangerous, meant he was hiding something, but I didn't know that this soon so I nodded. "Hi."

"We heard your folks was puke drunks, is that right?"

"Harris!" Glennis was walking on the other side of me and her voice snapped. "That's not polite, to talk that way."

"Well you can just blow it out your butt, you old cow. You ain't no grown-up to tell me what to do. How the hell am I supposed to know things if I don't go ahead and ask them?"

7

Glennis was a strapping girl, and she reached across my back and slapped Harris on the side of the head so hard his teeth rattled.

"You watch your tongue with all that swearing—I'll tell the folks and Pa will take a board to you."

But Harris ignored her—I would find later that getting hit hard by Glennis was a regular part of his life—and asked again, "Well, are they?"

I nodded. "They drink too much."

"Do they see stuff?"

"What do you mean?"

"I mean like old man Knutson in town. He's always drunk and pees his pants and he's all the time talking about seeing Jesus in a peach tree." He snorted. "Heck, there ain't a peach tree closer than a thousand miles to here—how can he see Jesus, even if Jesus was dumb enough to stand up in a peach tree? But like that—do your folks see things?"

I shook my head. "They just fight and then they puke."

"Hell, that's nothing. I puke all the time. Once I got the mad croup and I puked green for three, four days. Just as green as grass . . ."

We had been walking all this time and had reached the porch. The house was old and needed paint but was clean and looked somehow well cared for, comfortable. There were antlers nailed to the wall under the porch roof and an old shotgun rested in them and rubber boots were lined up near the door.

Glennis opened the door. "Straight in, then up the stairs."

I moved through the door into a small hallway with stairs at the end, and I climbed them to an unfinished upper floor that had been divided into two large rooms by a wooden wall. Outside it was beginning to become evening and dark, and inside it was hard to see anything at all. There didn't seem to be any electricity.

"I sleep out here," Glennis said, waving a hand at the room at the head of the stairs. "You're in with Harris . . ."

She opened the door and I carried the box through into the second room. There was a dormer window to let in some light but it was still dim and seemed raw. The rafters were exposed two-by-fours and the boards of the roof showed, as did the points of the nails that held the shingles. The floor was rough wood, nailed with framing nails.

The dormer window was in the middle and on either side there was a small iron bunk. On each bunk there was a mattress and pillow and quilt done in patchwork colors that didn't seem to make any sense or pattern, one color next to another.

"Yours is on the left." Harris motioned with his chin. "I'm on the right for now."

"For now?"

"I go back and forth . . ."

"You switch bunks?"

"Only when I need to."

"Need to?"

He studied me, his hands still behind his back, then he shook his head. "You don't know sheep crap from apple butter, do you? It's my guts. Kids' guts are like sheep guts. If a sheep sleeps on one side too long, all the guts squoosh over and stay there and it can't get up without it falls over. I always sleep facing the window in case there's a fire and so when I feel my guts get to squooshing over I switch bunks and sleep on my other side. See?"

I put my box on the left bunk and sat. "I guess so. Just tell me when we change . . ."

The mattress rustled when I sat on it and I poked it with my hand. "It makes a funny sound."

"It's dried corn shucks. These are from last year and getting old so's they don't sink anymore. You ought to hear it when they're new—it's so loud you can't sleep."

There was the sound of an engine and I watched out the window as the deputy backed the car out of the yard and drove off down the driveway. In spite of having done this many times I felt suddenly lost, alone, and leaned forward to watch the car leaving.

"Here."

Harris had moved closer to me and was holding something out in his hand. I turned from the window and looked closely—it seemed to be a green, somewhat slimy ball with legs and eyes. "What is it?"

"It's a frog."

He put it in my hand and I could feel that it was still alive. The legs moved. "What happened to it?"

"I shoved a straw up its butt and blew it up."

"Why?"

"So's it can't dive. You put 'em in the stock tank over by the barn and they float around on the top of the water and can't get down." He smiled. "Later I'll show you how to do it. You got to watch you don't blow too hard or they'll pop on you. I did it once and it took half an hour to get the frog guts out of my hair."

I put the frog on the sill of the dormer window where it rolled gently, its little front legs waving, and the deputy's taillights disappeared down the driveway.

2

Wherein I become a farmer
and meet Vivian

I was dreaming: random firing of neurons through my mind. Something about a fish and then a neuron shot through and it became a girl holding a fish and she was smiling at me, beckoning to me with the fish in an inviting way but there was a thumping.

Something thumping, jerking, shaking . . .

And I was awake.

It was completely dark, pitch black in the room, and for a few seconds I couldn't remember where I was. Then a faint light coming through the window revealed the walls, the bed, and standing over me the figure of Harris.

"Come on, wake up."

I looked out the window. "It's still night."

"Doesn't matter—the grown-ups have been coughing for fifteen minutes. Get your butt out of there or Louie will get all the pancakes."

"Louie?" Harris had turned back to his bunk and in one motion jumped into his bib overalls, hooked the suspenders. As previously the bibs were his only clothing. "Who's Louie?"

"He's just Louie. He's an old bugger who lives here and works. You would have met him last night 'cept he took the tractor to town to the beer hall. He came in during the night."

I remembered the night before now. I'd been given a plate of food because they'd already eaten supper and I picked at it in the hissing light of an overhead Coleman lantern without thinking or saying much while Glennis and Clair messed over the sink and stove. Then it was dark and we'd gone to bed. I'd tossed a bit but finally went to sleep, and I now recalled being slightly awakened by the sound of a loud motor coming down the driveway while I slept. A flare of lights passed the window and then nothing.

Harris came to my bed and jerked the covers back. "Get *up*."

With that he disappeared out the door and I heard his feet slapping down the stairs.

I tried to close my eyes and go back to sleep. It was black-dark outside the window and everything in me wanted, needed sleep. But another pang was there as well—hunger. I hadn't eaten much the night before. And then there was the curiosity as to who/what Louie was, and I rolled out and put my feet on the floor. It only took a moment to shuck into my jeans and pull a tee shirt on, lace up my tennis shoes, and head downstairs rubbing one hand on the wall to guide my way. But by the time I came out into the kitchen the table in the dining area was set and everybody was getting ready to eat.

As with the previous night the only light was from a Coleman lantern hanging by a wire from the ceiling. It sighed and burbled away, throwing a flat white glare on the table.

Glennis and Clair were at the wood-burning cookstove, turning pancakes. Knute and Harris were sitting at the table. Knute was drinking coffee from a mug, wrapping the cup in a hand that could have provided shade, staring at the table with a glazed early morning look on his face. Harris sat straight up, a fork in one hand, his eyes riveted on an empty spot on the table, his body half shaking.

At the end of the table sat an old man in a wool coat—though it was summer and hot in the kitchen from the wood stove on which the pancakes were cooking—a man so incredibly dirty that it was hard to find a patch of skin on his face or neck not covered with soil or grease. He wore a matted beard—

stuck with bits of dirt and sawdust and what looked like (and I found later to be) dried manure and dribbled spit and tobacco juice. All this around two piercingly blue gun-barrel eyes and a toothless mouth.

Louie.

I had seen bums in the city looking better and tried not to stare as I moved toward the table. Nobody spoke, just nodded and watched the pancakes cooking, and as I sat Louie took a metal can of Log Cabin syrup and poured it a quarter inch deep in a big puddle on his bare plate. Then he sat forward, as Harris was sitting, and watched the blank spot on the table with a fork in his hand.

There were two empty chairs and I stood for a moment until Glennis motioned to me.

"Sit. There by Harris."

I slid in next to Harris and assumed the other chair was for either Glennis or Clair. It didn't matter because neither of them sat nor did I ever see them sit to a meal while I was there. Clair cooked, stood over the stove and cooked, and Glennis carried the food to the table. I know they must have eaten but I never saw them sit down and eat.

Harris ignored me, kept sitting with the fork in his hand, staring at the middle of the table so that I wondered if he was in some kind of trance, perhaps not fully awake yet. Sleepwalking. God knows I was having trouble keeping my eyes open. There wasn't a clock anywhere but it felt like it couldn't be much after midnight and I figured at the rate things were going I'd be ready to go back to bed about ten o'clock in the morning.

I noted Harris grow even more tense next to me and looked up to see Glennis coming with a stack of pancakes on a plate. They looked delicious, steaming and fluffy, and I felt my mouth start to water.

I was not to get any of the pancakes.

Before the plate hit the table, Louie leaned forward like a snake striking and hit the stack of pancakes with his fork.

At the same instant Harris made his bid, jabbing for the stack with his fork but he was too late by miles.

The whole stack went to Louie's plate. Seven or eight of them dropped into the puddle of syrup, hesitated while he poured gobs more syrup on top of them, and then disappeared. With the possible exception of some species of sharks in a feeding frenzy, I have never seen anything eat like Louie. The pancakes were consumed whole. He deftly forked them in the middle, twisted them a half turn, and then speared them back into his toothless mouth letting his lips squeegee off the excess syrup, which then ran down into his beard, some of it to drip back onto his plate. In some wonderful manner he would then open his throat and swallow—all without chewing and only half choking.

The entire stack was gone in ten seconds flat, and he was sitting again with his fork in his hand, the syrup dripping from his beard down onto his shirt and lap.

"Rats," Harris whispered to me, sighed, and leaned back, shook his shoulders to loosen the tension, and got ready for the next batch.

Knute hadn't moved, was still wrapped around the coffee cup, and I stared at Louie in open admiration. He was a machine completely devoted to feeding itself. Not a word, no wasted motion—just strike and gone.

The next stack of cakes was the same except that Harris caught a corner of one pancake—a tattered remnant that he poured syrup on and ate carefully, chewing for a long time.

Louie ate the third stack as well—so far at least twenty pancakes—but he was slowing, dragged down by food, and when the fourth stack came he hesitated. Harris was ready, went in low and nailed it and put it on his plate—I thought with a low growl in his throat but I couldn't be sure. Louie didn't seem to mind and belched softly—a green drifter, the kind of belch that made people move away in a crowded room—and turned, waiting for the next delivery.

"Harris, you share now."

"But Ma . . ."

Glennis turned from the stove, leaned across the table, flicked at Harris with the back of her hand, and I heard her fingers connect with his forehead so hard his head jerked back.

He handed me a pancake.

"More," Glennis said. "Half." She raised her hand and he flinched and complied, although he tore the last one in two with his fork so I didn't quite get half of the whole stack. I didn't care. By this time I felt lucky to get anything and dripped syrup from the can onto my cakes—Harris had got to it before me and nearly drained it—and ate quietly.

Knute still hadn't moved except to raise his arm and drink the coffee. Glennis refilled his mug twice while we ate and he drained it both times without speaking.

"Come on," Harris said. "We've got to get the cows in."

He had finished eating and pushed back from the table. I still had half my pancakes to go.

"Let him eat," Glennis said. "He doesn't know how to eat fast yet."

Harris grew quiet but pulled at my shirt and whispered. "Come *on* . . ."

I ate as fast as I could—envy for Louie's technique grew strong in me—and still chewing followed Harris out the door.

Into pitch darkness. I had forgotten that it wasn't light yet and before I realized it I took a step off the porch and tumbled into the yard.

"Tarnation! Can't you even walk?" Harris dragged me up and disappeared in the darkness, headed in the direction of the barn.

The path proved to be an obstacle course. I tripped on a board lying on the ground, took a header over the yard gate, bounced off a granary wall, walked full on into a tractor, and finally arrived at the barn because Harris had taken pity on me and had at last led me by the hand.

I did not understand what "getting the cows in" meant. Or why we would want them "in." By this time I was swearing constantly, using words I had learned from soldiers in the Philippines and pretty much didn't give a damn (how I thought it) if I ever saw a cow—or Harris, for that matter.

Harris led me through the darkened barn—the smell of manure stopped me cold—and out the back door where he stopped and stepped off to the side and seemed to be fumbling with something. There was a rustle of paper, another moment of silence, and then a flare as he struck a match and lit a hand-rolled cigarette. He took a deep drag, inhaled, and blew smoke.

"A man likes a good smoke after he eats. You want one?"

In the glow from the cigarette he held out a cloth sack of Bull Durham with wheat-straw papers on the side.

I had never rolled a cigarette, had only tried smoking once—without inhaling—with my mother's cork-tipped Old Golds. But I wasn't about to admit it to Harris.

"Sure—give me one."

He had to light four matches to give me enough light to see but I at last got one rolled—a pitiful, lumpy-looking thing that threatened to fall apart. He lit the end of it with the flare from the fourth match and—not to be outdone—I took a deep drag, as he had done, and inhaled.

The effects were immediate and spectacular. The smoke went halfway down, I gagged, choked, and instantly lost all the pancakes I had eaten in a spray that nearly covered Harris.

He jumped back. "You don't know *nothing*, do you?"

In back of the barn was a quagmire of manure and urine, chewed into a perpetual muck by the cows, and I dropped the cigarette into this mess and leaned against the barn wall vomiting.

Harris retrieved the cigarette, brushed the burning end off, and put the remaining tobacco back in the sack. "This is hard to come by. I had to steal it from Louie and he's got eyes like a hawk. Come on, let's go get the cows."

He moved off in the darkness, walking barefoot across the center of the mud and manure, and I followed without thinking. In two steps I was in over my tennis shoes. I jumped back—cow crap to my knees—and tried to go around. Harris was out of sight in the darkness and I hurried to catch him, still dry heaving at five-second intervals.

There was the faintest gray light in the east by this time, and as I came around the side of the mucky area I made out a living form in front of me.

"Wait a minute. I don't know where . . ."

I was hit directly in the groin with such force that it lifted me off the ground, doubling me. I grabbed for the injured area as I started down, vaguely sensing that I was about to start puking again, and then something slammed into the top of my head and my world ended in an explosion of white light.

3

*Wherein Harris introduces me
to work and I meet Ernie*

The voices seemed to come from far away,
muffled and through a hissing ring.

"He doesn't know things, Harris—you
have to go slow with him."

"Well, how in the hell was I supposed to know
he'd walk right up Vivian's butt?"

Smack. "Watch the swearing."

"Well, what could he expect? Everybody knows
Vivian kicks and doesn't like anybody around her rear
end . . ."

"That's just it, Harris—he *doesn't* know. He's
from the city." I could recognize voices now, though
I hadn't opened my eyes. It was Clair. "He doesn't

know anything about farms, the poor dear. And what a way to start, getting kicked by Vivian."

Things were still blurred in my thinking. Somebody named Vivian had apparently kicked me. Hard. I made a mental note never to cross her again. Whoever this Vivian was, she had a very direct form of criticism. It was, however, strange that she would hide out in the darkness in back of the barn next to a pool of cow crap waiting to kick the bejesus out of people . . .

I opened my eyes.

I was in the small dining area next to the kitchen, lying on my back on the table with something wet and white over my head and eyes. I couldn't see anything.

"See?" Harris asked. "He ain't dead. He's moving—look at that. A big damn fuss over nothing."

Smack.

"If you don't stop swearing, I'll take a switch to you." Glennis's voice.

I raised a hand and felt a damp cloth on my forehead and face. At that moment the cloth was lifted away and I was looking up at Clair and Glennis. Harris stood down by my feet. Everybody but Harris had worried looks on their faces and I tried to smile.

"Are you all right?" Clair asked.

"I hurt." I touched my forehead where there was a lump that felt as big as a grapefruit.

"Yes, I know. Vivian kicked you. It always hurts when Vivian kicks you."

"Who's Vivian—and why doesn't she like me?"

Clair smiled. "Vivian is a cow, dear. And she doesn't like anybody. I believe she'd kick herself if she could figure out how to do it."

"Why doesn't somebody kick her back?"

Harris snorted. "I tried that once and she damn near killed me . . ."

Smack.

". . . Well, she did! I'm just saying what happened. You don't got to hit me for every little damn thing."

Smack. "It's the swearing, dear. You have to do something about it."

Harris turned to me. "You about ready to quit laying around? We're wasting daylight."

I tried to sit up but Clair held me down. "Not yet. Vivian caught you on the top of the head pretty hard. You take it easy for a little while. I'll get you some pie and a glass of milk and then we'll see."

Actually my head didn't hurt as much as my crotch but I couldn't tell her that so I just nodded. "Thank you . . ."

"Well, for God's sake—you're going to give him pie? For a little thing like that?" Harris shook his head. "Hell, I busted a leg and nobody gave *me* pie. I'll go out there and let that old bat kick me all day long if you give me pie for it."

The last words were rising in tone because Clair had finally had enough and she grabbed Harris and pulled him across the kitchen counter and pounded on his butt with a steel ladle. He wailed a bit but even I knew he was faking it and could tell that the whipping was having no real effect.

He ran outside as she dropped him. I rolled to a sitting position and resisted grabbing my groin and sat quietly at the table eating pie, which had a delicious tang that almost made the pain go away.

"You play slowly today," Clair told me as she and Glennis moved to the door with buckets, headed for the barn. "Don't let Harris talk you into anything wild."

"I won't."

And the thing is, I believed it. I really meant to take it easy, go slow, but as soon as they were out of the house Harris came in and stood next to me, fidgeting impatiently.

"Come on. We've got lots to do."

I followed him out, wiping the milk mustache off my upper lip, curious about the farm. The truth was I hadn't seen it during the daylight and had no knowledge of what was there.

Harris led off, headed for the barn where they were

still milking. The barn lay about fifty yards from the house and was made of old hewn timbers with a slanted corrugated-metal roof. To the right on the way to the barn was a board-sided granary and attached to one wall of the granary was the chicken coop. In front of the coop was a fenced pen and the pen was full of white young chickens—what seemed to be hundreds of them. There were other kinds of chickens loose all around the yard—fifty or so, pecking at the grass and scratching—and several dozen chicks following different hens, mimicking their mothers. The loose chickens were mixed red and black and spotted white, some with funny feathers on their heads that looked like pom-poms.

Various machines were lined up in a row beyond the chicken pen. Some I didn't recognize yet—a mower, rake, seeder, cultivator—but I knew what the tractor was, an old, green John Deere, and there was a tired-looking, caving-in truck with the Ford emblem on the radiator grill. Everywhere there seemed to be odd bits of junk and old machinery—mechanical arms that stuck up in the air, two old bicycles, or perhaps three or four old bicycles (it was hard to tell), rusting rolls of fencing, steel pipe, bits and pieces of old cars; it was like a junkyard.

Attached to the side of the barn were wooden pigpens, which seemed to be full of living boulders—enormous pigs that could have walked through the flimsy boards whenever they wished, or so it looked—and I was just going to ask Harris what kept them in when he stopped dead.

"Oh no . . ."

I had been following him closely and bumped into him when he stopped. He was scanning the yard and the area around the chickens, looking toward the top of the granary roof, which was to our right, and peering into and under the machinery.

"What's the matter?" I asked.

"I don't see him."

By this time I had figured Harris was pretty much invulnerable; it didn't seem that anything could harm him. But he was clearly concerned and I felt his uncertainty infect me. The hair went up on my neck. "Don't see who?"

"Ernie. I don't see Ernie. It ain't good when you can't see him."

"Who"—I looked quickly around—"is Ernie?"

But Harris wasn't listening. He kept scanning the yard and started walking toward the barn, walking so fast I almost had to jog to catch up to him.

"It's bad, me forgetting. It's 'cause you're here, of course, and you had to walk up old Vivian's butt and get a little kick and make me forget to watch . . . LOOK OUT!"

He had turned and was looking over my shoulder to my rear and his eyes grew wide. I half whirled, had a fleeting image of wings—huge wings, the wings of death—coming at my face and then Harris grabbed my hair and threw me down on my face out of the way.

"You feathered pile of . . ."

Harris was on his back, then on his hands and knees, and then on his back, rolling over and over, beating at what looked like a giant ball of dust and feathers and wings. This broiling mass of dust and profanity moved in the direction of the granary, bounced against the wall. I saw an arm shoot out of the middle and grab a piece of board and start beating the feathers until the dust settled and Harris was on his knees, holding the board with both hands, pounding on what seemed to be a tired feather duster on the ground.

"Damn you, Ernie. I'll teach you to jump me that way . . ."

I had risen to my feet gingerly—half expecting some form of attack from a new direction (it hadn't been a good morning so far)—and moved to see what Harris was beating on.

My movement distracted Harris momentarily and as he looked up there was a scurry of more dirt and feathers and his enemy disappeared in a hole under the granary floor. But not before I could get a look at it.

"A chicken?" I asked. "That was a chicken?"

Harris stood, threw the board aside, and brushed the dirt from his pants. "Hell, no—it's a rooster. Ernie. If you hadn't made me look up I would have killed him, too. He's been working on me for years. I just *hate* it when I can't see him."

I leaned down and peered under the granary, saw one yellow eye glaring back at me out of the darkness.

"He's got to jump me by surprise. In a fair fight I can whip him, but when you can't see him . . . that's the only way he can get me."

Now that the dust had settled I saw that Harris was scratched and torn in several places on his chest and one cheek. "You're bleeding."

He wiped the blood off. "It's his spurs. He gets to raking with them and it cuts some. I'd like to kill the old thing but Pa, he likes Ernie. Says he's good to keep the hawks and owls away."

I could believe that. I didn't know anything about hawks and owls but I sure wasn't going to tangle with him.

Harris was halfway to the barn and I hurried to catch up—not wishing to be left too close to the hole under the granary floor.

"We got to separate," he said. "And we're late."

"Why separate? Is there something else going to come after us?" I looked back, to the sides, half ready to duck.

"No. Not us, dummy. The milk. I thought I'd give you a chance to learn about the farm and the best way to start is separating." Harris paused to cough and spit and look away—a sure sign, I would find, that he was lying through his teeth. "The folks said to have you run the separator."

He walked in the double open door of the barn as he spoke and I followed him. I had never been in a barn during milking and was surprised to see that it was full of cows. Down the center was a clean, concrete-floored aisle twelve or so feet wide, with gutters on each side. On either side of this there were cows standing with their back ends to the aisle and it seemed like most of them were going in the gutter, which was already full of runny manure and urine.

The stench was overpowering—thick and fresh and so full of ammonia it clogged my throat and I had to wait a moment to get my breath before going inside.

As I entered, Clair came out from between two cows. She was carrying a three-legged stool and a bucket brim full of milk with thick foam on top, wearing a tattered old denim coat that hung in shreds. She smiled at me. "So you're up and about—feeling better?"

I nodded. "Just a bump on my head." I looked at the cows. "Is Vivian here?"

"Third from the end on that side." She waved. "Don't get near her hind end."

She walked past me and into a small room near the door and Harris followed. I turned but stopped. Louie was milking, sitting back in by a cow reaching up under her, and a huge cat, much larger than any cat I had ever seen, was sitting on its hind legs in the aisle in back of Louie. As I watched Louie directed a stream of milk at the cat's mouth and the cat swallowed it as fast as it came, waving its paws in the air.

Clair had dumped the milk in the little room and had come back out and Harris looked around the corner of the door. "Come on—don't you want to see this?"

Inside the room was a machine with two spigots. One fed into a large milk can and the other into a tall, thin bucket. On top of this device was a big stainless steel bowl full of milk and at the side was a wooden-handled crank.

"It's a separator. You put milk in the top and turn the crank and you get cream out of one spout and milk out of the other."

"Really?"

"Yeah." *Cough, spit.* "It's fun—want to do it?"

"Sure . . ."

I took the crank and started to turn, or tried to.

It seemed to be stuck, resisted my effort. "It won't turn."

"Sure it will. It just starts slow. Keep at it until it whines—then it'll be easy."

He grabbed the handle with me and helped and we kept at it and he was right. After ten or fifteen turns it started to whine and from then on it was easy, just a matter of keeping it going.

And going.

And going.

Harris waited until the handle was turning easily and then left, disappeared completely, and inside ten minutes I smelled the rat. They milked seventeen cows by hand, the four of them—Clair, Glennis, Knute, and Louie—and every drop of milk from all those cows went through the separator.

Which I kept cranking.

Each time one of them finished they came into the little room to dump their milk in the separator and so the level never seemed to go down in the big supply bowl on the top, and inside twenty minutes my arm felt like it was going to fall off. There was an urgency to it that took over—the milk, rivers of it, kept coming and I worried that if I didn't keep it up, they would just keep pouring and the separator would overflow.

The milk can on the floor began to fill and just as I worried that it would flow over Knute came in to dump a bucket of milk in the separator and re-placed the full milk can with an empty one. All without talking and I realized I hadn't heard him say a word since I arrived the night before.

Milking lasted perhaps two hours but it seemed a lifetime, an endless deluge of foamy-topped milk, a tidal wave of milk. Finally, when it seemed I could no longer move either of my arms and was seriously thinking of trying to use my foot, Harris came back in and grabbed the handle.

"My turn."

His timing was perfect. Clair came in with half a bucket of milk, poured it in the bowl on top of the separator, and smiled at me. "That's it—last one. Ready for a snack?"

I glared at Harris, realizing what he'd done to me. My arms hung uselessly at my sides, seemed so long I thought my knuckles would drag on the ground. "Snack?"

She laughed. "Sure. You didn't think all we ate was breakfast around here, did you? Lord, we'd waste away to nothing."

Harris did the last of the separating and the milk and cream cans were put in a water tank at the back of the small room to stay cool and we all walked back to the house.

Harris and I were walking in back of the grown-ups and Glennis, and I looked around for Ernie on the way back and Harris saw me and shook his head. "He don't come when there's big folks around—he's yellow clear through. Just a damn coward."

Smack. Glennis could hear a pin drop and she turned and whacked Harris across the head without missing her stride or her place in conversation with Clair.

In the house Glennis washed all the separator parts—disks and cones and weighted wheels—and hung them on wires on the porch to dry in the sun while Clair prepared the "snack."

It was a huge pan of sliced potatoes that had been boiled the night before for dinner and now fried in fresh grease with pepper, a plate heaping with bacon, and two dozen—I counted them going in the skillet—scrambled eggs.

The style was the same as at breakfast. Knute sat silently—I was beginning to wonder if he *could* talk—drinking coffee from a mug while Louie and Harris fought over food as it was brought to the table.

Louie's eating was different though still spectacular. He didn't use a fork but raised the plate and scooped sections of food into his mouth with his knife, again widening his throat in some way to swallow everything almost whole.

When the snack was over and Louie had used a piece of bread to wipe the grease from the serving plate, his own plate, our plates, and the frying pan, then pushed the bread into his mouth as he did the pancakes, letting the grease squeeze off and into his beard and down his chin—when it was all over I leaned back and tried not to throw up. It was delicious and I had more than overeaten. I was stuffed and thought seriously of going back to bed though it was only about the time I would normally get up. I was sure I couldn't move.

"Come on," Harris said. "Let's go play."

And he ran out the door.

I hesitated, wondering if I could get up, and Clair misread my inaction.

"Don't worry, dear—you go play. I'll call you for forenoon lunch."

I nodded and staggered to the door and heard Clair say to Knute:

"I like a boy with a good appetite, don't you?"

4

In which war is declared
and honor established

Harris stopped at the gate to the yard fence
—a combination of boards, nailed verti-
cally, and square-netted sheep fencing—and
studied the yard.

Ernie was near the granary, pecking and scratching with the chickens, and Harris nodded. "Good. He's
busy. You want to play war?"

I looked at the rooster. "You mean with Ernie?"
I didn't know for sure what Harris meant by "play
war"—maybe not the same as me, which was set-
ting up imaginary enemies and fighting them—but I
was pretty sure Ernie didn't take prisoners and I
wasn't about to play with him unless I had at least
a machine gun.

"Naw—the pigs. I pretend the pigs are commie japs and sneak up on them. You know. Just pretend."

"Commie japs?" I had lived in the Philippines a year after Japanese occupation and understood thinking of the Japanese as enemies but I had never heard the term *commie japs*. "What are they?"

"It's what Louie calls 'em."

"The pigs?"

"No. Louie almost went to fight in the war and he said the people he was going to fight were commie japs, so I just call the pigs that and then fight them." He moved toward the granary. "Let's go. I've got guns over here."

His "guns" were two narrow boards—one of which he'd used to pound on Ernie earlier—but with a little imagination they worked. I kept a wary eye on the rooster until Harris saw me and shook his head.

"Don't worry. He won't come at you if you see him. Only don't you see him, then watch it."

And so we went to make war on the pigs, Harris on the right, me on the left, keeping one eye over my back on Ernie should he decide to enter the fray.

Our enemies lay sublimely ignorant of our intentions, or so I thought, buried in a stew of mud with grain slop all over their noses, stomachs rumbling, grunting happily. There were three sows in one pen, a boar in another, and one sow in still another with ten or so piglets that were small enough to get through the fence if they wanted to.

"Look at 'em," Harris whispered as we made our assault. "Dirty commie japs laying there like they own the world."

I nodded. "Dirty commies." Which was at least partially true. They were, if possible, even dirtier than Louie.

"You ready?"

I nodded again, working an imaginary bolt on my board rifle. "Ready."

"I'll go right, you go left." Harris started for them in a crouch, gun raised, one foot slowly in front of the other.

"Left . . . ," I repeated, and mimicked his form.

My mistake was in becoming too intense. I'm not sure what I expected—maybe something along the lines of getting close to the enemy and then blasting them with heavy fire before they had a chance to escape. But I had a good imagination and inside of two steps they weren't pigs any longer. They were commie japs who wanted to rule the world and we were the only thing between their evil ambition and the true American way, and whatever Harris did I would back him up, I would follow.

And what Harris had in mind was hand-to-hand combat.

Ten feet from the pigpen Harris looked back at me, a strange glint in his eye, and silently raised an eyebrow in question.

I nodded, ready to follow him. Ready for anything. *Ready*.

He waved an arm in the classic infantry follow-me wave and screamed.

"*Arrrrrgggggh!* Die you commie jap pigs!"

He threw his board/gun aside, hit the pen at a dead run, vaulted over the low board fence, and leapt spread-eagled on the sows.

If asked later if I fully intended to follow Harris and jump into a pigpen, I would have denied it. You could smell the pig crap fifty yards from the pen. But this was war. My imagination had taken me, and caught up in the intensity of it all I was much too far gone to know what I was doing and I landed on the sows not two feet behind him, screaming something incoherent.

It is possible the sows had never been commie japs before—although since Harris lived there it's doubtful they could have missed out on such entertainment long. And it is also possible Harris had never jumped on them before in just this way, screaming and stabbing with an imaginary knife—although, again, with Harris there all the time it's doubtful. But I think it's fairly certain the sows had never been jumped on by *two* boys wielding imaginary knives, screaming death and mayhem at the tops of their lungs.

The effect was cataclysmic. Pig dung and mud went thirty feet in the air in a spray that seemed to block the sun and I learned—along with the fact that I had made a terrible mistake—something about basic physics: a lighter object, say a falling hundred-pound boy, cannot hope to move a heavier object, say a three-hundred-pound sow. Added to that was the realization that a sow covered in mud is too slippery to hang on to, and the final knowledge that the sows only *seemed* lethargic and were up and ready to do battle with any and all forces in less than a second.

We never had a chance.

I landed on a sow, grabbed, slipped, and was driven into the mud and pig crap by a hoof in the middle of my back. Out of the corner of one eye I saw the same thing happen to Harris—though he fought well on the way down, stabbing right and left—and then all was lost.

What actually happened is now blurred in confusion. I was up, Harris was up, I was down, Harris was down, we were pushed, pummeled, tossed and rooted, pounded into the muck, rolled into balls, and tossed like garbage back out of the pen.

"I'm blind! I can't see!" I screamed. I had pig crap *under* my eyelids. "Where are you? Harris!"

Something grabbed my hand and jerked, and I pulled back, thinking one of the sows still had me.

"It's me," Harris yelled in my ear. "Come on— we've got to get to the river." And he was laughing. "You look like a giant pig turd. Come on, let's get in the river."

A small river—little more than a creek, really— flowed along beside the farm in lazy S's that made shallow pools. Harris took my hand and dragged me through the pasture fence, across rough ground that kept tripping me, and into three feet of cold water.

I went down like a whale, sloshing back and forth, my mouth and eyes open—I had the muck inside my mouth as well—and didn't come up until all I tasted was water.

Harris was on the bank, dripping wet, rolling and slamming the ground with his fists, laughing so hard I thought he would choke.

"It wasn't funny." I said. "I think I ate pig crap."

"Minnie . . ." He choked back, trying to talk.

"Minnie?"

"Minnie . . . almost *died* when you landed on her . . ." He was off again, gasping and wheezing, and when I thought of the sow I landed on—apparently Minnie—and remembered her little pig eyes looking up at me as I came down, I started smiling, then giggling, and pretty soon both of us were rolling on the side of the river and we didn't stop laughing until I heard Clair yell something from the house.

Harris rolled to his feet. "Come on."

"What is it?"

"Lunch," he yelled back at me, running toward the house. "Forenoon lunch."

"But we just ate a few minutes ago."

"Did not. Hell, it's been close to an hour, maybe more. Come *on*—you want Louie to get all the cake?"

It wasn't a full meal—like the two breakfasts. There was sliced Velveeta cheese, some homemade bread, slices of meat (I found later to be smoked venison), pickles, and a large cake with chocolate frosting in a rectangular metal pan.

The problem was that the food was all sitting on the table ready for us and Louie was already there free feeding, so when we got there a lot of the sandwich fixings were gone and about half the cake, and Louie was sitting at the table with crumbs and bits of cheese and bread all over him. Knute was drinking another cup of coffee, staring at the table, and we ate silently, standing, dripping by the door, each with a sandwich in one hand, a piece of cake in the other.

Nobody asked why we were soaking wet or what we had been doing, which I thought strange until I remembered that they had been exposed to Harris much longer than me and were probably used to anything.

"The east forty is ready for mowing."

For a moment the words didn't register—seemed to be the voice of God talking. A deep voice, almost booming, and I actually looked up to the ceiling. Then I realized it was Knute. I stared at him but nobody else seemed to take notice, and he was still sitting, drinking coffee, staring at the same point on the table. But his words seemed to excite Harris, who smiled and went outside still eating cake.

I followed, licking frosting from my fingers, and caught him at the gate when he stopped to make sure he could see Ernie.

"What's up?"

"Pa's going to mow."

"So?"

"So we get to ride the team . . ."

"Oh." I had absolutely no idea what he was talking about. "Good. That will be fun."

". . . and hunt mice."

"Mice?"

"Man"—Harris shook his head—"you don't know *nothing*, do you?"

5

*Where I meet Buzzer and learn
the value and safety of teamwork*

Harris led me down to the barn and we had only been there a few moments when Knute came inside. He went to the back double-opening door and said quietly, "Bill, Bob, come on in now."

We were next to him and for a second I couldn't see who he was talking to. Then, from a stand of poplars close to the river, two huge gray horses walked out into the open.

I had seen horses in the Philippines, and in every western movie I went to, and knew about riding them. But Bill and Bob would have made two Triggers each.

They weren't just big, they were almost prehistoric—like two hair-covered dinosaurs walking slowly up from the river—and when they moved closer I could see that very little of their bulk was fat. Bunched beneath the skin on their rear ends and in their shoulders were great bulges of muscles.

Everything about them was massive. Huge heads that lowered to nuzzle Knute's hand while he stood in the back door of the barn, enormous round feet that sunk forever into the mud in back of the barn, great, soulful brown eyes that somehow made me want to hug the giants.

Knute turned and walked back into the barn and the horses followed like puppies. At the end nearest the front door was a double stall, and Bill and Bob moved into it. Knute came out of the pump house with a lard pail full of oats and poured half for each of them in a small wooden feed box nailed to the side of the manger.

Hanging on nails by the door were great loops of leather and chain with round collars over them, which I had seen earlier but hadn't understood and didn't want to ask about because I was sick of looking stupid.

Knute took the collars down and put them around the horses' necks while they were eating and then began draping the leather and chain over them, and I realized it was all harness.

Harris was all over the horses while Knute worked. He crawled under them, over them, handing ends of straps to Knute—who was back to silence—and the horses stood peacefully even when Harris stooped to walk between their back legs and out into the aisle to stand next to me.

Knute stood quietly until they had finished their oats. He then held their bridles loosely and, standing between their heads, backed them out into the aisle and walked them out of the barn to the row of machinery by the granary.

I got the impression that he didn't really need to lead them. They knew exactly where to go and what to do. When they came to what I learned was the mower they turned themselves around and backed, one on either side of a long wooden tongue, into position for pulling.

Knute hooked their trace chains into a big crosspiece of wood hooked to the mower and brought the tongue up to attach to a crosspiece from one horse to the next.

"Come on," Harris said, and I was surprised to see he was carrying an empty feed sack he'd picked up somewhere. "We got to get on."

"Get on what?"

"The horses . . ."

Harris jumped into the space between the horses by climbing on the mower and hopping along the tongue until he was even with their shoulders. Then he grabbed two horns that stuck up on top of the collar and climbed up until he was sitting on the right horse.

"Come *on*," he said. "Get up on Bill. You want to be left behind?"

As a matter of fact I was thinking that exact thing just then—that rather than climb up onto a horse as big as most trucks, I would definitely rather be left behind. But pride won out and I hesitantly made my way onto the mower in back of the left horse, Bill, and took one careful step after another to climb the tongue until I could pull myself up on his shoulders. He was so wide my legs seemed to go straight out to either side and I could feel him breathing beneath me like a warm bellows, great drafts of air as his shoulders worked slowly.

The ground seemed miles away and when I heard a sudden mechanical clanking and the horses moved slightly, I grabbed desperately for the horned things around the collar.

"Let go the hames," Harris said. "And raise your leg and put it under the reins. Pa can't drive with you sitting on the reins."

I turned and Knute had raised the sickle bar so it stood almost straight up and worked a lever to disengage it and was waiting patiently for me to do what Harris said.

"We want to hurry," Harris told me while I sorted my legs out from all the lines and straps and rings.

"We want to get out of the yard before Buzzer knows we're going . . . Oh shoot. Now it's too late."

I had just gotten squared away and was about to ask who Buzzer was when out of the corner of my eye I saw the cat come to the barn door and sit, watching us. "You mean the cat?"

Harris nodded. "It's better if we get out without him seeing us."

I had seen the cat briefly earlier, during milking when Louie squirted milk into his mouth, but I hadn't appreciated just how large he was; he was the size of a collie, maybe just a bit bigger, with large forelegs and huge, round pads on his feet. On the end of each ear there was a bedraggled tuft and his coat was spotted, almost dappled.

Knute steered the team toward a gate in a pasture fence that led us directly past the front door of the barn and Harris leaned across the space between the horses to talk quietly.

"You don't want to touch Buzzer."

I nodded. "You're right. I don't want to touch him." It seemed an odd thing to say since Buzzer was sitting down on the ground and I was what felt like eight feet in the air.

"He ain't normal or nothing," Harris continued. "Louie found him in the woods one spring when he was looking for wood to cut. Buzzer was just a kitten

48

then and Louie brought him back in his pocket. He grew some."

"I guess . . ."

I was going to say more but we were right next to the door and the cat suddenly bounced up—it seemed without effort—and landed on the rear end of the horse I was riding on.

I started, expecting the horse to react, but nothing happened. Bill just kept plodding on with Buzzer sitting on his butt, leaning out a bit to look ahead around me.

"No matter what he does, don't you touch him," Harris repeated. "Only Louie can touch him. Buzzer can be a little edgy about being touched if it ain't Louie."

I nodded and whispered to him, "Why is he riding on the horse with me?"

"He likes it when Pa mows 'cause he can get the mice. That's why I wanted to sneak out. He makes it hard to catch the mice because he's so fast. Just watch what I do and do the same. Sometimes we can get out without him if he's sleeping, but if he sees the mower he knows what's going to happen and he comes along and ruins it for everybody."

I wasn't sure what Buzzer was going to ruin—I couldn't, for instance, understand why we were going to get mice. As far as I was concerned Buzzer could have them all. I was ready to get off and let him have the horse as well.

Knute had stopped at the gate and Harris jumped down, opened it, closed it after we were through, and scrambled back up on Bob while we were still moving.

Once through the gate Knute turned the team and we walked slowly along the fence that went next to the driveway back out toward the main road. I kept a leery eye over my shoulder, watching Buzzer, but the big cat just sat there, looking at the sky and flying birds while the horses walked.

In a quarter mile or less we came to a stand of densely packed alfalfa almost waist high, and Knute stopped the horses at the corner of the field and lowered the sickle bar. He took a can of oil from a little holder beneath the seat on the mower and squirted oil all along the sickle bar, then sat once more and worked a lever to engage the clutch.

Harris got down and motioned for me to do the same. "We got to walk in back of the mower now and catch mice."

It was, finally, too much. "Harris, why do we want the mice?"

"For the money."

"What money?"

"Louie. He pays us a penny for each two mice we get him. Except for Buzzer, of course. Louie don't pay

Buzzer nothing 'cause Buzzer he just ruins 'em all to pieces and won't give them up anyway. Last summer I tried to take one away from him and get the money for it and he like to killed me. That's why I say don't you touch him nor take none of his mice."

"I won't."

I was going to ask why Louie paid for the mice— I thought, after watching at breakfast one and breakfast two and lunch, that he might eat them—but Knute made a squeaking sound by pursing his lips and the horses started forward, pulling the mower. With the clutch engaged, the wheels drove the sickle bar back and forth as the mower moved and sharp, triangular-shaped blades *snick-snicked* back and forth rapidly and cut the hay as neat as scissors.

I stood behind with Harris and watched the hay falling back across the sickle bar. The motion was mesmerizing. The bar slid along cutting and the alfalfa dropped and dropped in a never-ending row.

"Come on." Harris started following the sickle bar, walking eight or so feet in back of it. "Watch for 'em now, keep watching . . ."

I was more involved in watching Buzzer. He was between Harris and me, walking along, studying the newly fallen grass ahead alertly, taking one careful step after another. Suddenly he pounced, rising in an arc and down, with his feet buried in the grass. He brought one pad up with a mouse hooked in a razor-sharp claw, gave me what I took to be a threatening look, and popped the mouse into his mouth. If he chewed at all, it was just a single bite and down it went.

"Rats," Harris said. "See? Right there goes half a cent. He always gets 'em first. I think he hears 'em or something."

He waved for me to follow and I stepped forward, keeping well wide of Buzzer. Harris hadn't taken two steps when he jumped, forward and down, grabbed at the grass, and raised his fist clutching a handful of grass and a mouse. "Got one!"

I nodded but noted that Buzzer was watching as well, with a faintly proprietary air, and I wondered just which mice he might consider his and which he might consider mine.

For the time being it didn't matter. The alfalfa that fell back across the sickle bar was so thick I didn't understand how Harris or Buzzer could see mice.

I kept walking along. Harris got two more and Buzzer got three more and I still hadn't gotten any. Harris was starting to give me distinctly dirty looks and I decided I better get busy and had no more than lowered my eyes for another look than I saw a little form scurrying through the grass.

"Got one!" I yelled, a bit prematurely as I jumped for it. I missed, saw it wiggle again, grabbed at the grass, and felt the mouse wriggle inside my hand. I looked up and there was Buzzer—staring at me full on in the face with his wide yellow eyes. He pointedly looked down at the mouse, then up at my face again.

I nodded—"My mistake"—and gave him the mouse, throwing it to him. He caught it in midair and swallowed it whole.

"Ahh, come on," Harris snorted. He'd been watching the whole exchange. "That ain't fair—he didn't earn that one. He's just taking them from you."

"It's all right. I don't mind." I didn't, either. When he looked at me that way I would have given him anything he wanted.

"Don't be giving up so easy—that's half a penny every time you let him get away with it."

"You said not to take his mice."

"Well . . . just don't give up so blamed easy. He don't own the *whole* world."

I nodded to Harris and we continued, working through the morning. Harris caught just under thirty. I didn't do so well, first because I hadn't learned the trick of seeing them as well as Harris and second because of Buzzer. We worked out an agreement after a fashion. To wit: if I caught a mouse and he wanted it, I gave it to him. It turned out he wanted about two out of three mice that I caught, so when Knute pulled the team up in the shade of a huge elm and unhooked the trace chains and said, "Time for dinner," I had only put six mice in the bag. Three cents' worth.

"I'm not doing so well," I said as we sat under the tree and waited for Glennis and Clair to bring us what I would call lunch but they called dinner. "It's Buzzer. He keeps taking them from me."

Harris nodded. "He's a crook. That's how he got his name, sort of . . ."

"What do you mean?"

"We had an old collie dog somebody gave us last year. It didn't bother Buzzer none but Buzzer, he kept taking food from the dog. One day the dog got sick of it and bit him on the leg a little. That's how he got his name."

"From getting bit?"

"Naw—he killed the dog. Louie said it was like the dog got hit by a buzz saw. So we called him Buzzer after that. Just keep giving him mice. He'll fill up in a little while."

We sat, leaning against some rocks. Knute had taken the bridles off the horses, rubbing their ears and saying low things to them while he did, and they were eating alfalfa off to the side. I liked the sound of their chewing—it made the grass sound like it tasted good.

Knute rolled a cigarette and leaned back, dragging deeply. At the other end of the field I saw Glennis and Clair coming, carrying a double-handled boiler between them.

Harris stood. "Come on, let's help them." He took off running across the field and I followed, and we took a pail of water Glennis had been carrying in her free hand.

"Mind you don't spill," Glennis said. "There's just enough for the horses."

"Mind you don't spill," Harris mimicked, his voice singsong. *"There's just enough for the damn horses . . ."*

Smack.

He had forgotten himself. By taking the bucket from Glennis we freed up her right arm and she used it to pop him across the back of the head.

"Watch your mouth . . ."

He was unfazed. "You ever try that? Watching your mouth? It's impossible. You can't see your mouth without you have a mirror and I don't have a damn mirror . . ."

Smack.

We walked in silence until we came to the horses. I thought it was mean to hit him. He swore naturally, the way I had heard soldiers swear in the Philippines; swearing was a part of him. It was like hitting him for breathing. But it didn't seem to bother him to be hit.

The horses drank the way they ate. Their sounds

made the water seem delicious. We gave half the bucket to Bill and took it away to give the other half to Bob, after which they stood slobbering water and wiggling their lips before returning to grazing while we ate.

Clair and Glennis had carried what amounted to another full meal out in the boiler. There was sliced bread with butter, cheese, a big pot of beef stew, a whole round cake, three quart jars of rhubarb sauce, a large bowl of cookies, and a couple of two-quart jars wrapped thickly in feed sacks—one full of cool milk and the other full of hot coffee.

I thought I would still be full from the two breakfasts and the forenoon lunch but there was an edge of hunger there and I found myself eating right along with Harris and Knute. The food was so good it made my jaws ache to chew.

Neither Clair nor Glennis ate but sat picking at grass and talking softly, in a teasing way. Every once in a while Glennis would laugh softly and blush and Clair would poke her with a finger and laugh.

Knute leaned back and rolled and lit another cigarette when we were done and Harris flopped on the grass and burped.

"Good food," Knute said to Clair and Glennis by way of a compliment. He seemed about to say more but stopped and watched a hawk swoop low over the new-cut grass and I realized that Knute was always like that; always seemed about to say something but never quite got it out.

"I like field dinners," Harris said to no one in particular. "Especially when Louie ain't here. You don't got to fight so damn hard for food."

Glennis was too far away to smack him, sitting on the grass watching the horses, but she turned and threw a clump of dirt at him. "Watch your tongue."

He easily dodged and smiled, and I lay back on the grass at the edge of the field and watched small clouds moving across the sky overhead. A noise off to the side caught my attention and I rolled up to see Clair feeding Buzzer a scrap of meat from the stew pan.

She held it up pinched between her thumb and index finger and Buzzer delicately, with great care, used one needle-point claw in his huge foot to pull it from her fingers and place it into his mouth, the way he had done the mice.

"What kind of cat is he?" I asked.

Knute smiled but said nothing.

"We found a picture in a magazine looks just like him," Harris said. "What was that, Ma? What kind of cat was it?"

"He's a lynx," Clair said. "A big old puppy baby lynx . . ." Her voice got soft and you could see she wanted to pet Buzzer but she didn't touch him, and when she didn't feed him more, he walked away and began hunting the edge of the field looking for more mice.

In a little time Knute shredded his cigarette and put the leftover tobacco back in the sack and stood. The horses watched him, waiting, and he hooked them back up to the mower and sat in the seat and dinner was over.

Harris took the sack of mice and moved to the back of the mower and I followed and the afternoon went that way.

I got seven more mice for myself, Harris about forty, Buzzer six of his own and my other fourteen—he never did fill up. We ate again—Glennis and Clair brought out cake and milk and coffee and meat sandwiches—and then it was evening and we rode the horses back to the barn in time to help with milking. This time Harris took half the time on the separator, which was just as well because I was so tired I could hardly walk.

I vaguely remember eating another huge meal in the evening—watching Louie swallow what seemed like a whole chicken, bones and all—with heaping mashed potatoes, gravy, biscuits, and pie covered with whipped fresh cream for dessert. But I was so tired everything was fuzzy and things seemed to blur together.

After supper—what I would have called dinner and what seemed like the tenth meal of the day but was really only the sixth—everybody went into the dining/sitting room and sat in chairs while a clock on the wall ticked, and I went face down on the table and started to sleep. I simply couldn't keep my eyes open.

"Poor dear," Clair said. "He's a little tuckered . . ."

I felt somebody lift me, smelled Knute's tobacco, and I was carried upstairs and laid on my bed, fully clothed. I kicked out of my shoes and pants, and the events swirled in my head as I lay back in the dark.

I'd been kicked in the testicles, slammed in the head, worked at the separator until my arms seemed about to fall off, narrowly averted disaster with a manic rooster, wrestled commie jap pigs in a sea of pig crap, ridden horses as big as dinosaurs, had a losing relationship with a lynx, eaten eighteen or twenty meals, and helped to capture mice for God-knows-what purposes.

And I'd been there one day.

I tried to open my eyes. (I'd heard Harris come in the room as I flopped back and I needed to know the answer, was *dying* to know the answer: why did Louie want the mice?) But it was impossible. My eyes didn't open, a wave of exhaustion roared over me like a soft train and I was gone.

6

*Wherein I learn some more physics,
involving parabolic trajectories,
and see the worth of literature*

A daily routine evolved in the first week that
was to carry me through my entire summer
with Harris and the Larsons: up while it was
still thick dark, watch Louie feed and try to compete
and get a little food, out to help with milking—
searching carefully for Ernie on the way—eat again
when milking was done, and then get in trouble.

It wasn't that we tried to get in trouble. Indeed,
Harris and I did not think in terms of trouble at all.
It's just that many of the things we wanted to do—
well, perhaps *all* the things we wanted to do—seemed
to cause difficulties in some way that we had not
expected.

A good example of this theory is the problem that

happened because of the Tarzan of the Apes comic book.

Part of my treasures, along with the "dourty peectures," was a goodly supply of comic books. Some of them were not so good. There were, for instance, two Captain Marvel comics that I didn't like. But among the better ones—Superman, some good Donald Ducks, and a couple of really good Real War comics—there was my favorite, a Tarzan of the Apes bonus edition with a story about Tarzan in the lost land of dinosaurs, where he trains a triceratops to ride by hitting it on the side of the snout with a stick.

Harris shared my enthusiasm for the comics. This interest would diminish slightly when he came to see the "dourty peectures," but by the end of the first week he hadn't seen them yet and *had* seen the comics, including the Tarzan of the Apes. His reading wasn't up to my level but it was good enough and the pictures gave him enough information to fill in the gaps.

"That guy was something," he said, closing the comic book. We were sitting in the open granary door. I was watching closely for Ernie, whom I hadn't seen for over fifteen minutes—usually a very bad situation. I now personally had been attacked by Ernie several times, the worst inside the outhouse. It faced the river, away from the house, and so the door could be open and it was fun to sit there and watch things down by the river while I was going to the bathroom. Ernie had sneaked around the side of the outhouse and jumped me right in the middle of—well, just say that it was very lucky I was sitting on a toilet when it happened—and during the ensuing fight (really, just me trying to get out of the outhouse alive) it looked like the toilet had been hit by artillery.

So I watched closely for him and never went out in the yard without a board, which I was holding now.

"He never seems to touch the ground . . ."

"What?"

"Tarzan," Harris repeated. "He don't never touch the ground. He just swings in them trees on them vines unless he's riding one of them big gooners . . ."

"Triceratops."

". . . Whatever. He still ain't touching the ground, is he?"

I thought about it. "No, I guess not."

"Might ought to be a good way to live, just swinging around. *Hmmmm.*"

And herein lay the one shining ability of Harris—he believed everything was real. When he went for the pigs they weren't pigs, they really were commie japs, whatever that was in his mind.

When he read a Tarzan comic it wasn't just a made-up story. It was real. He thought in real terms, in a real world, in real time. The only instance I saw this vary was when I found out why Louie wanted the mice.

The day after we'd mowed and gathered mice I'd asked Harris why Louie needed mice.

"For coats," he'd said. "Little coats."

"Coats?"

"It's better to show you. Come on."

He had led me to the granary. The downstairs of the building was arranged in wooden bins full of oats and barley and some wheat. Upstairs there was a rough wooden floor and a crude ladder on the side wall leading up through a hole. Harris moved up the ladder like a monkey and I followed, still trying to imagine what he could be leading me to.

Upstairs there was a big cleared area and in the middle of this a large wooden table—ten by ten feet, easily—was set on thick wooden legs.

"See?" Harris said. "Here's why Louie needs the mice . . ."

The table was covered with small carved figures. At first I couldn't understand. There were men and horses and little cabins and small trees and teams of horses pulling sleighs full of logs.

"It's a winter logging camp," Harris said. "Louie is always carving on it."

"Wow . . ." It was incredible. There were

dozens, *hundreds* of little men working at different aspects of logging, cutting down little trees with axes and small two-man saws, building little cabins, riding little sleighs, sitting in little outhouses. And every horse had gray fur and many of the men were wearing gray fur coats. "He skins the mice to make coats and horsehair," I said, "for this?"

"Yup. Pretty slick, ain't it?" He had shaken his head. "It's all just little carvings. I think he does it because he's got brain worms. Got 'em when he worked up in the Oak Leaf swamp digging drainage ditches when he was young. That's why he does 'em— of course, they ain't real. It's all in his head."

It was the only thing Harris didn't think of as real and I was fascinated by Louie's dream world. I had gone up there several times since and looked at the table and still hadn't seen everything and, indeed, was thinking of climbing up there again now to look at it once more but I noticed that Harris was studying the barnyard with new interest.

I hadn't been there long but I knew when he had that look—it seemed the corner of his right eye went up slightly and it gave him an almost evil gremlin appearance—it meant he had a new idea. Sometimes they were good ideas, oftentimes they were bad ideas, but they were never, never boring ideas and always worth interest.

"What are you looking at?"

"I'm wondering," he said, "what Tarzan would have done had he lived on a farm."

"I don't think he . . ."

"Do you s'pose he would have had to touch the ground?"

"I don't see how he would have . . ."

"Or do you s'pose he would have been able to swing all through the barnyard without touching the dirt?"

He stood and left me and went around to the back of the granary and chicken coop and in moments returned lugging what seemed to be half a mile of thick hemp rope.

"I've been looking," he said, dumping the rope at my feet. "And it seems to me that a man could make it from the granary to the loft of the barn without touching the ground, then from the loft back over to that hayrack. We just tie the rope to that elm limb there and over there to the oak limb. Look, see there? If we get to the hayrack, there's even a place where we can swing out over the river, if we have enough rope for it."

I was looking at the rope. It seemed ancient, so old there was mold and mildew growing on it. "I don't know . . ."

"Come on, there's nothing to know about it. I'll just shinny up that elm and you throw me the rope and we'll do her."

He was gone in an instant and halfway up the tree before I could say that I thought the rope would fall apart.

"Up here—throw me the rope." He had crotch-ridden out on the tree limb and was beckoning down to me. He seemed a mile up and I had to throw the rope several times before he caught it. In a minute he had it tied to the limb with what appeared to be eight or nine knots and had dropped the end to the ground and climbed back down.

I tested the rope gingerly at first, then hanging on it with my full weight, and finally bouncing. It held but had spring to it, a little stretch.

"Here, hold it like this and when I get on the granary roof flip it up to me."

"How are you going to get on the granary roof?" I asked but he was gone again, a dust cloud coming up in back of him as he ran into the granary and disappeared.

He reappeared almost instantly at the small window in the peak of the granary roof. It opened inward and he pushed it over and wriggled until he was half in and half out, then he turned, reached up, and grabbed the peak of the roof and pulled himself up.

"Give me the rope."

I whipped the rope sideways several times and finally managed to get it close enough for him to grab it.

"Way it works is I'm going to swing from here over to the loft door on the barn and just whip inside and drop in the hay."

On the front of the barn there was a large opening for putting hay inside to store for the winter. The door opening was seven or so feet wide and the big door was tied open to ventilate the loft. Inside there was an old pile of hay left from winter.

"Are you sure you want to do this?" I called up.

"You bet. And as soon as I do her you can try it."

I had pretty much made up my mind that there was nothing on earth that would get me to "try her"— Harris looked like he was a mile away, sitting up there straddling the peak of the granary—though I was completely willing to help Harris.

He stood, wobbling on the peak, his bare feet holding at the hip and ridge, and held the rope. I eyed the swing it would take to make the barn loft, and while there was still some doubt I nodded up at him to give him confidence. And in truth I thought he might make it.

Yet there were several mistakes that had already been made that would alter Harris's destiny. Wind, humidity, rotation of the earth, stretch of old rope, and springiness of an elm tree limb—all had been ignored in the computations. But worse, far worse— I had laid my board/weapon down and we had both forgotten Ernie completely.

"What did he always say?" Harris yelled down to me.

"Who?"

"Tarzan, you dope. Isn't he always saying something when he does this?"

"He has a yell."

"How does it go?"

I did a Tarzan yell, or a version of it. "Like that."

"When he swings?"

"That's what it says in the comic books."

"Well, then. Here goes."

He started a Tarzan yell and without any hesitation whatsoever jumped off the granary roof into space hanging on to a rotten piece of hemp rope.

We would argue later over many aspects of the Tarzan Leap, as it came to be known. How far it went, how far off the aim really was, how much Harris meant, and how much (I thought all of it) was accident. One of the main points of contention involved the yell.

Harris claimed it was a valid and authentic Tarzan yell, made as he swung down from the roof. I maintained that it became a scream of terror the moment his feet left the granary and that, coupled with Ernie's enthusiasm, was the reason for my own sudden involvement.

In retrospect there was no one point that it fell apart but many smaller disasters that fed the big one.

Ernie had been hiding under the combine. I was standing a few feet off the line of swing with my back to the combine, not twelve feet from the lurking Ernie.

As Harris began his swing, Ernie saw his chance—saw that I had put my board down and was concentrating on Harris.

Just as Harris stepped off the roof Ernie hit me in the back of the head and drove me forward nearly into Harris's path. Rope stretch and poor aim did the rest. Harris veered enough to hit me head on, Ernie still riding me and spurring me. I grabbed at Harris—I would have grabbed at anything to get away from Ernie—and hung on as the momentum of Harris's swing carried me, and the clinging Ernie, along for the ride to the barn loft.

Or what should have been the barn loft. Here again miscalculation intervened. Harris's original swing was off, slightly, to the left. My weight and drag brought it more to the left—as did Ernie's raking and clawing—so that all of us were well off the expected flight path for the loft; were, indeed, aimed perfectly for the pigpens.

The rope almost held us. That we agreed on. And it would have held Harris alone just fine. But the weight was more than doubled with me hanging on to him.

We swung in an arc—Harris, Ernie, and me—back

off the ground, directly over the pigpens and the by-now panicking sows.

Where the rope broke.

We hit in a plume of mud and pig dung—I had the foresight from past experience to close my eyes and mouth this time—propelled by the swing and gravity, with a force that knocked the wind out of me and for an instant even seemed to stun Ernie.

Our surprise arrival did not stun the pigs. They ran over us like stampeding cattle, then back over us, then over us again, and seemed to be thinking of making it a regular part of their exercise when I heard:

"Come here, you gooner!"

Out of the corner of my eye I saw Harris—never one to waste an opportunity—hit one of the sows on the side of the snout and swing up into the saddle and I thought, as I went down in a new wave of tromping pig feet, that he looked almost exactly like Tarzan riding a triceratops—if Tarzan had worn bib overalls and been covered with pig slop, of course.

7

In which I am exposed to the city,
and the lure of the silver screen,
and orange pop

Summer days fed into summer nights full of
fireflies and the smell of lilacs around the
house and back into days where the farmyard
became a whole way of life. Any concept of an outside world was lost in the endless games and new
ideas Harris conceived.

But when I'd been there two weeks—long enough
so that the other parts of my life were all but forgotten and I was content to stay there and play forever—a day came when there was a change in the
routine.

Actually the day was much of the same. Up, worry
about Ernie, help with milking, and get in trouble.

In this case the trouble involved playing at being what Harris called "a red Indian."

Definitions are important. I had often played Cowboys and Indians back in the cities where I lived, and played War a great deal in the Philippines, and had ironed out forms and disciplines for both games. In War you were always the hero and you always won and you always were generous with your foe—if he lived. In Cowboys and Indians you were always the cowboy and always won—usually with as much gunplay as possible—and often saved somebody in the winning.

Harris had not had other children to play with as much as I had and so he had to make up some of his own rules.

There were, for instance, no cowboys the way Harris played. This caused some difficulty because I had a revolving cylinder, silver-plated (chrome, really) six-shooter with me. I had not used it for War because it was the wrong kind of gun but it made me, clearly, king of the cowboys. It was hidden in my box beneath the bed, along with the pictures, and I suggested bringing it out but Harris was adamant.

"No. There ain't no cowboys. Only red Indians. And don't nobody win but the red Indians."

This idea was new but I was willing to try it as long as I didn't have to lose. What with Ernie and the pigpen I had been doing rather a lot of losing lately.

"What do we do?"

"We lurk," Harris said, "and shoot the hell out of everything."

I warped my imagination around and figured a way a red Indian could have come up with a silver-plated six-shooter—something to do with barter and some ponies—but Harris again shook his head.

"You never in your life saw no red Indian with a silver six-shooter."

"Well what do we shoot with—our fingers?"

It was a lesson to me—to never, never underestimate Harris.

He took me around to the back of the granary. There had once been a chicken pen back there, years and years before. It had all fallen down and rotted away but willows had grown where the chicken yard had been. Fed by the chicken manure the willows had gone crazy and made a stand of perfectly straight limbs so thick it was almost impossible to get through them. They were every size from as thick as a little finger to one inch across.

Harris pulled a butcher knife out from beneath the granary. It was Clair's favorite meat knife and only that morning she'd wondered where it had gone and I knew then that Harris had planned to play red

Indians even yesterday. I was pretty sure that Clair wouldn't want Harris to have the knife—or anything with sharp edges or a point, as far as that went—and said as much.

"There's too blamed much of that in the world," he said.

"Too much of what?"

"Rules. Every time you turn around there's something you can't have or something you can't do. I'll tell you what"—he looked at me and waved the butcher knife—"you never in your life saw no red Indian putting up with rules, did you?"

Which was perhaps true. But it was entirely possible that no red Indian had ever taken Clair's butcher knife and hid it under a granary either, I thought, yet I didn't say anything.

He waded into the willows and started whacking away. The thicker willows became bows and the thin ones became arrows. We worked for an hour or more peeling bark and using heavy sack-cord as string for the bows and stripping the bark from the thin ones to lighten them up for arrows.

We sharpened the arrows—each of us had six—and set out to do as Harris had stipulated: lurk and shoot everything.

Here Harris and I differed dramatically. I thought he meant, literally, *things*. I was content to shoot at dirt hunks, mounds of hay, clumps of horse droppings—and just pretend they were settlers or cow-boys or cavalry.

Harris took it to the next highest plane of realism and went for living objects—cows, horses, and pigs.

I hesitated. Clearly this violated some rule or we—as I pointed out to Harris with what I thought to be impeccable logic—would have seen the grown-ups out shooting at the animals with bows and arrows.

"They won't see us anyway," Harris pointed out. "We'll be lurking."

He convinced me. Not directly, but I had started to consider the secondary benefits of this approach. The truth was I had two formidable enemies at the farm. One was Vivian, who had driven my testicles up somewhere around my tonsils and my head down between my shoulders. I still twinged when I thought of her. The second deadly adversary was, of course, Ernie.

It was all right to play red Indians and imagine enemies, I thought, but how much better to have real enemies to shoot at.

We lurked.

Harris led off and I followed, mentally awaiting my chance to get a shot in at Ernie or Vivian, who was out in the pasture in back of the barn.

Harris shot at the sows. I shot at the sows. The

arrows bounced off their sides without hurting them, though they squealed and acted in other ways just like surprised cavalry.

Harris shot at a chicken. I shot at a chicken. We both missed—chickens being a much smaller cavalry than pigs—and undaunted we headed around the back side of the barn. I was watching to the rear, hoping for a shot at Ernie, and turned to the front just in time to see Harris take a quick shot.

There had been a small patch of gray fur by the edge of the corner of the barn, not much bigger than the palm of my hand, so small that Harris would normally have missed. And he would probably have missed, but he shot instinctively and his reflexes carried the day.

This time he hit perfectly. The sharpened point plunked into the center of the fur and there was a screech like somebody drawing a million fingernails across blackboards and about fifty pounds of really angry lynx looked back around the corner directly into Harris's eyes, his soul.

"Oh . . ." he had time to say. "Buzzer. No, Buzzer. I'm sorry, Buzzer. I'm really sorry. Buzzer, no! Please, Buzzer . . ."

He had thrown down the bow and by this time was running across the yard trying either to make the granary or the house. It didn't matter which because Buzzer was on him in three bounds and the two of them went rolling in a cloud of dirt and screeches.

"He's killing me!" Harris screamed. "Help me!" Arms and legs and paws and tufted ears seemed to be everywhere.

I was worried about Harris—though I didn't think he could be killed by anything—but I wasn't about to cross Buzzer. I yelled, "Buzzer, you stop that now . . ."

Which of course had no effect at all. The fight kept roiling and boiling, and I'm not sure what the outcome would have been but suddenly the screen door on the house swung open and Clair was standing there, her hands in her apron.

"Harris! You quit playing with Buzzer now and come inside—we have to get ready for town."

And that stopped Buzzer. When the dust settled he was standing on top of Harris, looking at Clair, spitting out bits of bib overall, his stump tail wriggling happily.

"Get off me, you gooner," Harris said. "Didn't you hear? We got to go inside . . ."

He rolled out from under Buzzer and stood. His bibs were in shreds and he was bleeding from a dozen or so cuts but seemed in one piece and he ran to the house. I made a loop around Buzzer, who spat once more and went back toward the barn, and I followed Harris into the house.

"Is there a dance or what, Ma?"

Harris was by the sink where Clair was pumping cold water into a steaming pan of hot water to cool it.

"Yes. There's a dance and a party for the Halversons—to help them rebuild. Their house burned."

"Is there a picture show?" The tragic news didn't seem to bother Harris much. "Do we get a picture show?"

She smiled and nodded. "I think so, yes."

"Can we have pop?" he added. "Don't we get to have pop for the picture show?"

She didn't answer that one but instead bent his head over the sink and started cleaning it in much the same way she or Glennis cleaned the separator parts after milking: pouring hot water on a spot, scrubbing with a stiff-bristle brush until he screamed—or actually well after he screamed, ignoring the cries for mercy and some first-rate profanity—and then doing another spot.

I stood watching all this, not thinking that I would be next, until Harris was done—literally and figuratively—and then Clair turned to me.

"Put your head over the sink, dear—you look like you've been swimming in manure."

I did so and in moments understood why Harris had screamed so hard. It felt like the brush was made of nails. She dug and probed at every crevice and opening on my head, pouring scalding water between bouts of scrubbing until I felt like all my skin was gone.

"There," she said, pouring water the color and consistency of the Mississippi down the sink from the dishpan. "Now you're clean. We'll go right after chores, so you two stay clean and change clothes after we milk."

Harris went out the door at a run, jumped off the porch down into the grass, and ran around in circles, prancing like he was riding a horse. "Maybe it'll be Gene."

"What are you talking about?" I was still hurting from the scrubbing and felt to see if any of my ears remained.

"Gene Artery, you dope. Didn't you hear what she said? They're going to have a movie show. There ain't but about three picture shows in the world and one of them is Gene Artery."

"You mean Gene Autry?"

"Right. He runs around shooting things and he never misses. You ought to see it. He can shoot the gun clean out of somebody's hand and never a miss. Man, I hope it's that Gene Artery picture show. I've only seen that one fifteen or twenty times and it gets better each time. He's got this fat guy runs around with him who's dumber than a pump handle and is always getting into trouble. I don't see how he stays alive from one picture show to the next . . ."

"It's a movie."

He stared at me.

"It's not new each time. They just do it once and then they show it all over the place." I had seen Gene Autry movies many times, and others, Roy Rogers, some war movies.

He snorted. "Sure. You must think I'm as dumb as the fat guy. Heck, you can *see* them moving each time. Don't you suppose I know what's real and what ain't?"

He just didn't understand and I thought to explain it more except that it was all a bit fuzzy for me as well. I knew about movies and all but I wasn't exactly sure how they were made—not certain enough to take a lot of questions. Besides, a secondary consideration had arisen that had me puzzled.

I was sure we were well into the middle of a huge wilderness. In all the drive up here with the deputy, we hadn't passed a town or a road to a town and I couldn't for the life of me understand why they would have a motion picture theater in the middle of the forest.

"Where do they show the movies?" I asked. Harris had completely ignored Clair's warning and was playing in the dirt where we had a couple of old iron toy tractors and had made a farm.

"On the wall," he answered. "Where else? Don't you know nothing?"

So I dropped it, thinking I would find out soon enough.

It was an hour until we milked—which seemed a week—and another hour after we finished milking and separating to eat supper and change clothes. After wolfing food—almost but not quite keeping up with Louie—Harris ran upstairs and changed. He came down in moments with clean bibs on—still without a shirt, without shoes, and the side buttons open on the bibs showed he had no underwear on. I put on a clean tee shirt and came downstairs to find that even Louie had dressed for the occasion. He had changed shirts—not to a clean one (I don't think anything he ever wore was clean) but a different dirty one.

Knute and Clair and Glennis were all fresh and clean—Knute was wearing a newly ironed work shirt and I realized I had seen Clair ironing it two days before, heating the iron on the back of the stove and pressing a bit at a time.

Knute drank another cup of coffee, then nodded and without speaking went outside, leading the entourage to the truck.

The truck was old—*how* old was and is open to

conjecture. As was the actual make. It had been patched and rebuilt so many times with so many different parts that it might have been a Ford or a Dodge or even a Chevrolet. Whatever it was, it had been dead for a long time and Knute kept it running with a Lazarus approach, a mixture of miracle and work.

It didn't have a battery and we all stood watching while he cranked it, advanced the spark a bit, cranked it again, advanced the spark a little more, and cranked once more. This time it kicked so hard it nearly broke his arm. He swore eloquently—I began to understand where Harris found his ability—and then backed off on the spark, cranked once more, and it started with a sound like the pistons were exchanging holes.

He stood, smiling, and we all clambered in. That is, Glennis, Clair, and Knute got in front. Louie climbed in the rear of the truck and sat on the bed, his back to the cab, and Harris and I joined him.

I still had no idea where we were going but everybody was so glad to be doing it that I fell in with the enthusiasm.

"We don't get to town that often," Harris screamed—a full bellow was necessary to override the sound of the engine. There was no muffler at all and very little tailpipe. What pipe there was ended at the front of the bed so the full din of the engine came up around us. "It's the best thing there is, especially if we get some pop to go with the picture show . . ."

I got about every third word and he had to translate over the engine sound and he finally gave up.

Knute turned right at the end of the driveway and we started driving—*ricocheting* might be a better word—down a mud track that went through miles of forest.

When we'd done this for half an hour we came into a clearing a mile across—hacked out of the forest the way Knute's farm had been cleared—and in the middle of this clearing stood four frame buildings and a tall sheet-metal covered grain elevator. A set of railroad tracks ran alongside and past the four buildings.

Harris smiled widely and pointed. "Town."

I said nothing, but the way it looked reminded me of nothing so much as some villages I'd seen in the Philippine Islands—a scattered collection of huts thrown in the middle of nowhere.

We bounced across the tracks, turned on a dirt road that went in front of the buildings, and stopped in front of a clapboard-sided shanty that seemed about to fall in on itself. It had no windows in the front or the sides but an open door and a crude wooden porch across the front. Above the door in rough, hand-painted letters were the words:

LUMBERJACK LOWNGE

The other three buildings looked much the same except one of them had a glass window in the front and was apparently a dry goods store.

I couldn't for the life of me see what everybody was so excited about. There were already six or seven trucks parked in the street—not in any order, just left where they stopped, as Knute now did with our truck—and as the engine died with a gasp, a thin boy about my age walked out of the door and onto the porch. He was holding a bottle of Nesbitt's orange pop and as soon as he saw our truck he turned and tried to get back in the door.

He was far too slow.

"Hunsetter, you gooner!" Harris bellowed as he piled over the side of the truck. "Where the hell is my aggie shooter?"

Harris bounced once on the ground and landed on top of the boy. Orange pop sprayed in the air as they went down and rolled into the street in a cloud of dirt and curses. It was a view of Harris I was becoming accustomed to, and I was wondering if I should help or get a bucket of water or pry them apart with a stick when Clair took my arm.

"Come on inside, dear. They'll be in when they're done playing . . ."

It was becoming evening and the room was dark— the only light came through the open door—and it took a moment for my eyes to get accustomed to the dim light.

When they did I saw a plank bar down the left side of the room with no stools, three tables on the right with benches instead of chairs. At the back of the room there was a small wooden platform next to what I took to be a back door. On the platform there were two fiddle cases and an accordion so big it seemed that it would take two men to play it.

The room was full of people, all of a set piece with us—clean but in rough clothes. The women in starched dresses, the men in overalls. There were young people scattered here and there, all drinking Nesbitt's orange pop. Glennis and Clair waved at somebody and went to sit at the tables while Knute and Louie went to stand near some men at the plank bar.

I knew nobody, but for the moment it didn't matter. I was watching Louie.

He drank like he ate. A man in the back of the bar—also dressed in bib overalls, although he was wearing a tie with his work shirt—gave Louie and Knute each a tall, dark bottle of beer. Knute took a drink and put his down to speak to a man next to him but Louie stared straight ahead and simply upended the bottle and pushed it in to the back of his throat and drained it, licking the bottle opening dry with his tongue when it was empty.

He set it on the bar and the bartender brought him another one. He did the same. He kept doing this until I felt a tug at my sleeve and turned to see Harris.

"I *hate* a gooner that will steal a marble from a man . . ."

He looked some the worse for wear, being scuffed and dirty, and one suspender of his bib had come undone, but he was holding up a large cat's-eye aggie shooter marble with pride. He dropped the marble in his pocket and moved to the bar to stand next to Louie.

I followed and was going to ask what had happened to the other boy when I saw him come into the room. He was in worse shape than Harris, seemed to be dragging a leg and favoring one arm and was bleeding slightly from the nose, but had about the same amount of dirt on him and moved to stand with some grown-ups and ignored us.

Harris looked up at the bartender and waited, and in a moment he handed us two orange pops. No money changed hands. I never saw any money for anything, beer or pop, pass over the bar and I thought it must be free but Harris corrected me later.

"It's writ down. Clel's got him a notebook in back

and he writes everything down. I'd like to have half what's on that notebook—you could own every marble in the world."

We stood by the end of the bar, not far from Knute and Louie—who were talking horses and crops to the other men at the bar. Or at least Knute was. Louie was drinking beers whole just as fast as Clel the bartender could bring them.

"He'll pee hisself later," Harris said, noting that I was watching Louie. "Just comes in the top and goes out the bottom like a pipe . . ."

Presently three men separated themselves from the rest and without speaking or further ado mounted the platform, picked up the instruments—the smaller of the men hoisting the accordion with a short grunt—and began playing.

It was barely music—sounded more like cats fighting inside a steel drum—but it was very loud and had a steady rhythm, and soon couples were dancing.

Harris ignored the adults and kept watching the back door—or what I took to be the back door—with a steady intensity.

We had gone through our pop and been given new ones, and as soon as Clel handed us our pop he started walking down the bar aimed for that door.

"Come on." Harris grabbed my arm. "We want to get good seats . . ."

It was not a back door but the door to a storeroom. I followed Harris in—blinded by more darkness yet—and could vaguely make out a room full of beer crates stacked around the sides. In the middle on a rickety wooden table was an old motion picture projector and on the wall a sheet had been hung.

Harris dragged me to the center of the room and pulled two beer crates up to sit on, directly to the side of the projector, then waited impatiently, holding his pop with both hands, while Clel and a dozen or so other young people came into the room.

In the dim light from the door, Clel went to a box of what seemed to be car batteries on the side of the room and hooked two wires to the terminals with alligator clips. The projector came on and its beam of light hit the sheet with a dazzling glare.

Clel worked in silence while we sat waiting, feeding film from the old reel through the projector with many clicks and jerks, hooking it to the take-up reel.

Then he hit a switch and the projector started up with a noise not unlike the old truck that had brought us to town and on the screen was a picture of Gene Autry riding and shooting.

It would be wrong to call what we were watching a movie. I had been to many films by that time and recognized that there were problems with this one. The credits and probably the first fifteen or twenty minutes of the film were gone, lost over years of showing. The picture just jumped into the middle of the story with Gene riding Champ and shooting at somebody, and when the reel ran out—some thirty minutes later—he was still riding Champ and shooting at somebody. Though it was a talking film there was no sound equipment, so it remained silent and any idea of story line from dialogue was lost. The whole film was devoted to Gene riding Champion and shooting at something, with one scene where he played a guitar and sang and another where he jumped off a saloon roof onto Champion and rode away, either escaping some men in the saloon or trying to catch some other men who had run off.

Then the reel ended with the screen going flash white again.

"Damn." Harris snorted. "I just hate it when it ends that way . . ."

As if on cue Clel came back in carrying a dozen bottles of orange pop in a wooden case. He handed us each a bottle, then rewound the film and started it over and went back out front where the music was getting louder and more incoherent all the time.

And the children all sat and watched it again as if seeing it for the first time.

I leaned forward to whisper in Harris's ear: "Isn't there another reel?"

"What?"

"You know—of film. Isn't there another reel?"

"Not unless you want to watch the news about the war. Clel's got that one but it's really short."

"The war?" The Second World War had been over for nearly five years.

"Yeah—with the commie japs and all. They're fighting like dogs over there. But it still ain't this good. Now shut up and watch the picture show . . ."

He turned back to Gene and we sat through another showing of the film.

When it was done Clel reappeared with orange pop, rewound the film, and started it over.

And over.

And over.

On the fourth showing I couldn't stand it any longer and I left the back room to watch the goings-on in the front before I fell asleep.

The room was lit by two Coleman lanterns hanging from the ceiling and full of smoke and sound. The music had gotten much louder and there was a smell of beer and sweat. It seemed that all the married couples—like Knute and Clair—were dancing in the small center of the room, leaving the tables empty, and all the old men like Louie were standing at the bar.

Some of them were talking but Louie was silent and still drinking the way he had before—a whole bottle at a time. He looked almost the same but there was a glazed look in his eyes that hadn't been there before, and I did a little quick figuring and decided that if he'd been drinking at the same rate all along he was probably well into twenty or thirty bottles by this time.

I looked and, as Harris had said, Louie had peed his pants.

I moved toward the tables to sit and watch the band and as I walked past the end of the bar Clel magically appeared and handed me another orange pop. This made me remember my bladder was bursting. There was no bathroom inside so I went to use the one outside and stepped into total blackness and nearly broke my neck and the bottle of pop, falling from the porch.

In a moment my eyes became accustomed to the dark, and I saw that there were several young couples standing in pairs, holding hands, talking quietly. It took me some time to find the outhouse and use it and come back inside.

I sat at a table, sipping pop and watching them dance, and within a few minutes they slowed the music to a waltz and it seemed absolutely impossible to keep my eyes open.

I lay my head down on the table and closed my eyes, just for a moment, and everything from the day caught up with me and went sliding together, and within moments I was sound asleep.

I'm not sure how long I slept. When I opened my eyes Knute was carrying me in one arm and Harris in the other. He put us gently in the back of the truck. I closed my eyes and awakened a moment later to see Knute carrying Louie out to put him in the truck as well. Louie was as stiff as a ramrod, his hands still holding the last bottle of beer he was drinking.

Then not even the noise of the truck could keep me from sleep.

8

In which we educate two horses,
and I learn that the one blamed
is not always the one guilty

N ow you be like you was the fat, dumb guy
and I'll be like I was Gene."

"I don't know—there's a lot that can
go wrong . . ."

"Come on—didn't I sit last night and watch Gene
do this very thing seven times?"

"Well . . ."

"When's the last time I was wrong?"

I started to say something about hitting Buzzer
in the rear with an arrow but it didn't come out. The
truth was I thought what Harris wanted to do would
work.

Sometimes even the grown-ups could make mistakes. Usually it was us, but on several occasions

that summer they took leave of their senses and left us completely alone.

This was the first time. All of them, including Glennis and Louie, had gone to the Halversons' to help clean up from the fire and we had been left alone at the farm.

"You bring the cows in and set up the separator when it comes time to do chores and we'll be back in time to milk." Clair had paused with her hand on the truck door, seemed about to say something else—I thought to warn us not to burn the house down or start a war—and then changed her mind.

And they drove off down the driveway.

Harris stood watching the truck leave, innocence all over his face, until it was out of sight, and no sooner had it turned onto the road a quarter mile away than he was running to the barn.

"Come on."

"What are you going to do?"

He hadn't spoken but grabbed Bill's halter out of the barn and went into the pasture toward the work-horses. This was when we still could approach them—later in the summer, for reasons that will become obvious, they wouldn't let us come closer than thirty yards before moving off.

Bill gently lowered his head for Harris to put the oiled leather halter on and lead him to the barn.

To be totally honest I knew by this time that we

were going to do something wrong. It was not that we always did something wrong—I hadn't, for instance, shown Harris my "dourty peectures" yet—but this had *wrong* written all over it. I was pretty sure we weren't supposed to be messing with the horses, and the combination of Harris and a two-thousand-pound workhorse simply had to be wrong.

"You're always wanting to play cowboys," he said. "Well, go get your little silver pistol and we'll play cowboys."

Bill came along peacefully and Harris, looking like an ant leading a rhino, led him through the barn and approximately ten feet out the front door.

Harris looked up. "That ought to about do it."

"Do what?"

"Get him right for when we jump on him."

"We're going to jump on Bill?"

"Yeah. Like I said, you be the fat guy and I'll be Gene and we'll jump out of the loft door onto Bill and ride off after the rustlers."

And as I mentioned, I thought we could do it. Oh, not at first. At first it looked a lot like jumping off the granary roof holding a rotten piece of rope or leaping on a three-hundred-pound commie jap sow.

But Harris pointed out that it wasn't that far down to Bill and that he had a broad back made of largely soft flesh and that we rode him all the time when he was pulling the mower and that in any event there really wasn't any choice because Gene did it in the picture show and we *had* to do it or we'd forever be lower than pig crap . . .

So I agreed.

The problem came about because of Harris's lack of understanding of the nature of falling bodies.

We went ahead—Harris with enthusiasm, I with some residual dread—and set up the scene. Bill was put into position and an armload of hay placed in front of him to keep him there, head down, munching peacefully.

We then climbed into the loft and moved to the front door and looked down.

"See?" Harris said. "His back is like a big kitchen table down there . . ."

In truth Bill looked small, too small to hit, but Harris didn't give me much time to think.

"The way we'll do her is I'll swing out a bit on the dump rope and you just jump on down. That way I'll hit him up on the shoulders and you come in back of me and we'll ride off and save the rustlers."

"Get the rustlers," I pointed out. "You don't *save* the rustlers, you *get* them."

He stopped. "What's the difference? We still jump on the horse, don't we?"

I nodded.

"Well, then, don't be so quick to talk when you don't know what the hell you're talking about." He grabbed the dump rope that hung down from the overhead rail and was used to pull hay up into the loft and backed off ready to run and swing out over Bill. "You ready?"

I nodded again but it was a lie.

"Say it."

"Say what?"

"Heck, don't you know nothing? You're the fat guy. Aren't you supposed to say, 'Let's go save the rustlers'?"

"I don't know."

"Say it."

"All right."

"Say it *now*."

"Let's go save the rustlers."

Harris nodded and ran out of the loft holding on to the dump rope.

Caught up in the enthusiasm I actually started to follow him.

Right here several things went wrong.

First off, even if Bill had seen the movie he might not have tolerated two boys jumping out of a barn loft onto his back. But he hadn't seen the movie and so the plot line was a complete surprise to him.

Then cowardice took over and at the last minute I tried to stop. I was already half out of the loft door and I wheeled in midair and grabbed back at the edge and barely caught myself to hang there like dirty laundry and watch the events unfold over my shoulder.

Harris was less fortunate.

He held on to the rope too long and released when he had already started swinging back toward the loft door.

He missed Bill's front end and came down squarely on the horse's enormous rump, which was, unfortunately, actually as wide as a kitchen table. Harris's legs shot out sideways and his groin crunched with a sound I could hear from where I hung.

"Oooomph!"

He grabbed himself and started to slide off Bill's back end.

Bill, in the meantime, did exactly as a horse should do when something out of nowhere jumps on his back. Horses have reacted to predators jumping on their backs for millions of years in one specific way. They buck hard and when the predator is dislodged they kick the bejesus out of it.

Bill obeyed the genetic codes in his system and bucked as Harris hit him, driving Harris back up almost even with the loft door opening where I still hung.

Harris, legs straight out to the side, holding his groin tightly, did an almost perfect backward swan dive and was coming down on his head directly in back of Bill where he would have crunched in the dirt and chicken mess.

But Bill obeyed the second code and just as Harris came into range kicked with one back hoof, a hoof as large as the top opening of a milk bucket, with a force just below nuclear.

It caught Harris directly in the middle of the stomach and drove him backward into the barn so hard that I heard him skip twice across the barn floor.

I hung from the door opening another second while Bill went back to eating quietly. Then I dropped and ran into the barn.

Harris was by the back door, having been propelled nearly the full length of the building. He was on his side, still holding his groin, looking past me at Bill, or trying to. His eyes had a distinctly unfocused look and he was still fighting for breath.

He whispered something so softly I couldn't hear.

"What?" I leaned closer.

He mumbled again.

"You'll have to talk louder . . ."

He got a breath down and hissed. "Did we save the rustlers?"

I didn't have the heart to tell him the truth. "Yes, Gene. We saved them."

"Good."

He mumbled something else.

"What?" I leaned closer.

"Don't move me for a while."

"I won't."

"Good."

It was during the next week, after another Saturday night dance and the ensuing Gene Autry binge, that we tried the second cinematic event. It was also coincidentally the second time the grown-ups left us alone, this time to take a load of hay to the Halversons.

Again Harris watched them drive off, this time with the old John Deere tractor pulling a trailer of hay and everybody sitting on top holding pans of food.

As soon as they were out of sight he headed for the barn and took down Bob's harness and moved into the pasture.

Bill would not let us get close but Bob hadn't been indoctrinated—yet—and Harris walked up to him and haltered him and led him to the barn.

"I'm not jumping out of the barn loft on him," I said as Harris led him through the barn and outside into the yard.

"Naww. We've already done that. What's the other thing he does?"

"Who?"

"Gene, you dope."

"Sings."

"Naww. We ain't gonna sing. It's the other thing."

"Well he rides, and jumps on horses, and sings, and . . ."

"Shoots," Harris interrupted. "He rides and shoots, don't he?"

"Well, yes . . ."

"He's got that horse going wide open and he pulls out that six-shooter and blasts away, don't he? Well don't we do that we're lower than pig puke, ain't we?"

"That's what you said last time. When we jumped out of the loft and you got kicked through the barn."

"When *I* jumped," Harris corrected me. "You hung and *I* jumped. Could be if you had jumped the right way instead of turning into a chicken it all would have worked out all right. You scared to do this?"

Of course that did it. I *was* scared—any time Harris started talking about shooting and horses it would be impossible not to be scared. Which of course meant I had to do it, whatever it was he wanted to do.

"Here's how we'll do her," he said after he'd put a bridle with short reins on Bob. He was leading the horse across the farmyard and near the house. "You get that silver shooter and I'll get a gun and we'll climb up on Bob and get him moving at a good clip and then we'll shoot."

"A good clip?" I had seen Bob and Bill trot. Once. Other than that they never did more than a lumbering walk. "Can't we just walk?"

He snorted. "Don't you watch them movies at *all*? You ever see Gene walking his horse while he shoots? Now run get your gun . . ."

I ran in the house and upstairs where I had the cap gun. There were no caps but I was good at making gun sounds and I thought it was just as well. The sound of the caps going off might startle Bob and if we got him moving at all I didn't want to startle him. Ever. Memories of Bill line-driving Harris through the barn were still fresh.

I found the cap gun and turned and trotted down the stairs and onto the porch and stopped dead.

Harris was already on Bob, sitting well up on his massive shoulders, and he was holding a gun easily as long as he was tall balanced across his lap.

"What's that?"

"What's what?"

"That gun—that's a real gun."

"Oh, this? This is Pa's old twelve gauge." He shrugged airily and coughed and spit to the side. "He lets me use it all the time."

This was such a blatant lie that it didn't deserve acknowledgment.

"Come on—you going to wait all day?"

He maneuvered Bob close to the porch and after

three jumps I managed to wiggle up and sit in back of Harris, my cap gun in one hand.

"You ready?"

I nodded, then realized Harris was facing forward and couldn't see me. "Sure . . ."

He raised both feet straight out and slammed his heels into Bob's sides so hard I heard wind whistle out of the horse's nostrils.

Bob stepped forward, one, two steps, barely walking out of the yard as he moved up the driveway.

"We got to get him moving. Here, you kick when I kick . . ."

I wasn't all that sure we wanted him to run, but I still rankled about that fear business so I started flailing away with my heels as Harris did with his and Bob moved first into a jarring trot and finally into a lolloping canter that had almost no real speed but must have triggered seismographs all over North America.

Dirt clods, rocks, bits of gravel flew up and Bob managed to move into something close to a full gallop. I had never been this fast on a horse and it was exhilarating. We seemed to be using up the driveway at a phenomenal rate and I took aim at a fence post off to the side and made gun sounds and shot, then over to a rock, back to another fence post.

Heck, I thought, *this isn't so hard.* I relaxed my grip around Harris a bit and let myself get into the roll of Bob as he galloped—forgetting that it seemed twenty or so feet to the ground—and there I was, shooting Indians and rustlers and thinking maybe I really *was* a cowboy, when the whole world exploded.

Harris had swung the shotgun out over Bob's head, directly between his ears, and let go a round of high-base goose load—what would now be called magnums—with number two shot.

I'm not sure who was the most surprised—Bob or me. I had no idea Harris had loaded the shotgun with a live round and I *know* the thought had never entered Bob's cranium.

The recoil from the old goose gun was staggering. It drove Harris back, into me, then me back, and both of us off Bob just at the same moment Bob stopped dead—his ears no doubt whistling—then wheeled much faster than I would have thought possible for a creature of his size and tore back to the yard directly over the top of both of us.

We were scuffed some and I couldn't for the life of me figure up from down for a moment or two, but worse, Bob had stepped on the shotgun and broken the rear stock in half.

"Shoot." Harris stood, staring down at the shotgun. "Glennis is gonna kill me."

"Glennis—what about Knute? It's his shotgun."

"He won't say nothing. Just look at me. That's

bad enough but Glennis, she's going to take a hoe handle to me."

I nodded. Glennis was something to be feared. I had seen her hit Harris so hard the snot flew when she just wanted to check her swing and wasn't even seriously mad. I shuddered to think what she could do if she was really upset.

"Well, there's nothing for it . . ."

I nodded again. He'd just have to face the music.

". . . you'll have to take the blame."

"Me?"

He nodded. "It's the only way out of this."

"Glennis will kill me."

"Naww. She don't hit nobody but me and a guy named Harold Peterson. He up and touched her on the chest at a church picnic and she brained him with a hot dish casserole. I think she's sweet on him though because she helped clean the casserole off while he was laying on the ground . . ."

The injustice of it all rankled me. I had done plenty wrong on my own without seeking new blame. "I'm not taking the blame for the shotgun."

"It ain't like we got a choice, is it?"

"I've got a choice."

"It's this way." Harris gave me a speculative look. "If you got a choice, I've got a choice, too."

"What do you mean?"

"If you make a choice not to take the blame, I

might make a choice to tell about them pictures you got in the box under the bed."

"You snake! You've been in my stuff."

He shrugged. "Not so's you'd notice. I just looked at 'em once. Well, maybe more than once. It's kind of fun to look at 'em. Makes my business feel funny and I start thinking about Shirley Everson . . ."

He had me. I understood that but I still fought a bit. "I ever catch you in that box again I'll beat the tar out of you." It was a hollow threat and he knew it but he had the decency to give it to me.

"I won't. And don't worry. Glennis ain't going to hit you and even if she does, it won't be like she'd hit me."

The irony was that I lied the best I could, looked them all straight in the face, told them how I found the shotgun and took it out and found a shell in the cabinet (Harris coached me) and loaded it and felt just awful about it and Glennis patted me on the head and turned and hit Harris so hard he almost somer-saulted out of the kitchen.

"What was that for?" Harris asked, staggering back into the room.

"For not stopping him," Glennis said. "He could have killed himself with that old gun."

"Well damn . . ."

Smack.

Harris was right about one thing though. Knute never said a word, just looked at me and then went out to glue and wire the stock together. But that look made me wish I'd never lied about anything in my whole life.

9

Where I learn of play,
and strength, and raw work

It sometimes seemed all we did was play that summer—and to be sure, most of what Harris and I accomplished centered on playing. Or trying to play.

But a goodly portion of our time was given over to work and it was during work that Knute broke his hand and I saw how Glennis really felt about Harris.

After haying was done all the hay had to be either stacked or pulled up into the loft to be stored for winter use. Knute used the horses to mow the hay and rake it up with a curved-tine dump rake that left it in piles. Then he used the tractor with a kind of big basket on the front to go around picking up the piles to push into the hay stacker. The stacker had another basket on the front that took the smaller piles and threw them up and over the back to make larger stacks.

The stacker was pulled up and over by either Bob or Bill, and Harris said when he was small he used to ride them while they were working, pulling forward and backing up.

I thought it might be fun to do but neither horse wanted me close. I guess they thought I had something to do with Harris jumping on them or shooting off their backs.

But we had work to do anyway. As the hay came up over and down from the stacker we had to use forks to spread it out evenly and then walk around packing it down.

Initially, on the first day, it was fun jumping and bouncing in the fresh summer hay. But that only lasted for part of the time it took to make the initial stack. Then there was another stack, and another, and soon it was work, hard work in dusty hay on a hot afternoon.

By the end of that beginning day of stacking hay I was exhausted and could hardly keep my eyes open to eat the last meal of the day.

On the next day, and the next, the work ground me down to the point where I could close my eyes and see haystacks looking like huge loaves of bread in the fields. And even jumping down from a little platform inside the barn near the roof to pack the hay so we could put more in became work.

Haying took a week and at the end of it I was numb. But there came a day when the endless hay at last ended, not a wisp of grass to put up, and Harris looked at me standing by the barn and said:

"Last one in the river sucks sour pig mud . . ."

And we were gone, racing for the river at a dead lope, Harris shucking his bibs as he moved, gaining the advantage because that's all he wore.

The river ran past the house and barn, and near where it passed the house there was a bend and a small pool where eddies had cut the bank. It was not deep—four feet at the most—but had a sandy bottom and was clear and cold, and we hit the water running. Or Harris did. I had to stop and take my shoes and pants off.

While I was doing so I heard a thumping sound in back of me. I thought immediately of Bill and Bob and worried that they were coming to join the party but I turned to see Knute coming, pulling off his bibs and unbuttoning his shirt.

He was a big man, not fat but wide, and when he got his clothes off he looked as white as paper except for his face, which was burned red.

Harris was already in the water and I was in midair when Knute went over me and almost drained the pool when he landed. Water must have gone twenty feet in the air. He was going so fast he almost skipped across the surface, and as soon as he came up he grabbed Harris by the arm in one hand and me in the other and started slamming and flipping us around like a couple of dead fish.

Then he threw us to the side and walked out of the pool and dressed, putting his clothes on over his wet body, and walked up to the house without saying a word.

Harris came up covered with mud, sputtering, and I looked around the pool trying to understand which way was out of the water.

"Man," Harris laughed, "ain't it fun when Pa plays with us?"

"Plays?"

"Yeah. He hardly ever does it. I just wish he'd do it more. I think it would settle him some."

It felt like most of the bones in my body had turned to cartilage. At no time during the "play" did I ever have any idea of control over my own body and I had never felt strength like I felt in Knute's hand holding my arm, or the ease with which he flipped us around. His grip was like a vise connected to spring steel.

"Settle him?" Knute seemed the least nervous person I had ever seen. He just drank coffee and smoked Bull Durham cigarettes.

"Yeah. It's his nerves, makes him the way he is.

Worry about the farm and all. He used to play with me all the time. Once he threw me clean over the threshing machine. *That* was a day, I'll tell you."

"I'll bet . . ."

We were lying nude on the bank of the river, the sun cooking us dry. I kept looking up toward the house and covering myself with my hand—we were in plain view—but Harris didn't seem to care.

I lay back and watched the clouds for a moment and wondered how it could be that I was living here now and had been living somewhere else before, and why I didn't seem to remember so much of the other place I had lived, and wondered if I could talk about it with Harris, when he suddenly swore.

"Damn."

"What's the matter?"

"Tick."

"Wood tick?" I opened my eyes and sat up. We'd been seeing ticks all summer. It was now about the first of July and they were almost all gone. Clair once said that the ticks were always gone by the Fourth of July. "So what?"

"Not wood tick. *Fever* tick."

I scanned the ground around me carefully. "They'll give us a fever?"

"Not us, the cattle. It means we'll have to dip the cows. Man, I hate to dip cattle."

"Dip the cows?" I had no idea—as usual—what he meant. "How do you dip cows?"

But he ignored me and instead slipped into his bibs and headed for the house. "Come on, we got to tell Pa about the tick."

At first it didn't seem that dipping the cattle would be such a difficult thing. There was a large pen in back of the barn with a gate that was usually left open. Feed was put in a trough and it brought the cattle into the pen. The cows came readily enough but there was a bull, a large, flat-sided, black-and-white Holstein that kept pushing at the fence, throwing dirt up over his shoulders and blowing snot.

"He looks mean," I said to Harris. "The bull."

"Naww. He's just nervous. We've kept him apart until now and he knows it's time to be with the cows. He don't like nothing to mess his breeding up. And he don't like to dip. None of 'em do."

With all the cattle in the pen and the gate closed, a chute was rigged up with board panels and a ramp that led up to the top of a long sheet-metal tank over four feet deep. Inside the tank another ramp was laid that led out of the tank. It had wooden crosspieces so the cows could get footing to climb out to yet another ramp that led down to the ground and out into the pasture.

The idea was simple. The cattle were to be pushed out of the pen into the chute, forced to jump into the tank, and then prodded up the ramp to freedom.

"What goes in the tank?" I asked.

"Creosote," Harris said, spitting. "Stuff makes blisters come on your skin so's it looks like you've got a sickness. Try to stay clear of it."

I made a mental promise not to get anywhere near the tank—completely forgetting the concept of fluid displacement and just exactly what happens when a half-ton animal jumps into a tank of liquid.

While we spoke Knute and Louie backed the old truck up to the tank and tipped fifty-five-gallon drums of evil-smelling liquid off the bed so they would run into the tank until it was nearly three-quarters full. Clair and Glennis had come from the house to help but stayed well away from the dip area.

Then Knute stood by the tank and looked at Harris and nodded. "Let 'em go."

Harris opened the gate leading from the pen into the chute and stood back as if expecting the cattle to just run and jump in themselves.

Nothing happened.

"Aww heck." Harris climbed into the pen, motioning for me to follow, and—staying well clear of Vivian's back end—we shooed and pushed on the cows until one of them started into the chute.

As soon as the first cow was close to the tank

itself Louie reached across and grabbed her tail and twisted it over, hard, and the cow made a jump forward that carried her over the center of the dip tank.

She hit with a splash like depth charges going off. Creosote dip flew ten feet in the air and came down on all of us, and I immediately felt a burning sensation where it hit bare skin.

There was no time to worry about the creosote because while we were getting the first cow going Clair and Glennis yelled from the outside of the pen and got the rest moving to follow the first one.

It was fast work for ten or fifteen minutes. Cow after cow jumped in the tank, nudged by Louie's tail-twisting trick, and Knute pulled a mop out of the back of the truck and mopped creosote over the top of each cow as it hit the tank.

Finally there was only one left—the bull. He followed meekly enough, was almost in the position where Louie would grab his tail when he hesitated.

I was standing off to the side in the pen, halfway through the wire to climb out. I happened to be looking at Knute and when the bull stopped, seemed to wait just half a second, Knute dropped the mop and started to move.

I thought I had never seen a person move so fast but the bull was faster. He wheeled around, turning on himself *inside* the chute, and headed back out with a low bellow that made the ground shake.

And there was Harris.

He had been bringing up the rear, pushing the rest of the cows into the chute, and had actually come a slight way into the chute himself. He might have had time to do something, climb out of the chute, run. But he was looking down to step forward over the fresh cow manure that filled the chute and the bull was so fast, faster than even Knute, that Harris didn't have a chance.

The bull hit him like a train, driving him back into the pen and down. It was all so powerful and sudden that I didn't have time to yell, to do anything but stand with my mouth open.

Knute was over the fence and on the bull in not more than a second. I saw it, saw it all as if it were in slow motion, but I still didn't believe it.

He grabbed for Harris, snatched him somehow from beneath the bull's head, pulled him out and up and threw him over the fence toward Clair and Glennis, where he landed like rags.

Then Knute hit the bull. I'm not sure where, somewhere on the head or nose. He raised his right hand and brought his left up and clasped the two hands together in one fist and brought them down on the bull, brought them down like a mountain falling, hit him with a sound like an ax chopping a watermelon.

And the bull went down—bellowed and goobered

snot and spit and dropped on his front knees—and Knute stood with his left arm hanging at his side, bent funny just above the wrist.

He took two steps past the bull to the fence near Clair and Glennis and threw a leg over the wire.

"Is he all right?"

"I don't know." Clair was rubbing Harris's chest, her forehead wrinkled with worry. "That damn bull. I told you to get rid of that thing . . ."

Harris looked dead. I had seen dead people and Harris looked dead to me and I still hadn't moved, still stood in the pen by the fence, and I wasn't sure if I was shocked by what the bull did to Harris or from hearing Clair swear.

But it was Glennis who surprised me. She stood looking down at Harris for a moment, her hand halfway to her mouth, then she fell forward onto her knees across from Clair and held Harris's head and made quiet crying sounds and spoke to him.

"You come back, Harris. You come back now. We don't want you gone. You come right back and I'll never whup you again so help me God . . ."

Whether it was Clair rubbing his chest or Glennis holding him or just that he couldn't be killed—which I thought—Harris's legs moved and he raised his arms and his eyes opened and he looked up at Glennis.

"What the hell happened?"

Her hand came up but true to her word she didn't smack him and in fact her vow lasted a whole day, until late the next afternoon when Harris tripped on the edge of the porch and ripped a strip of blue words that almost peeled paint.

As soon as he was all right Clair left him with Glennis and turned to Knute.

"Your arm," she said. "You hit him too hard."

Knute nodded. "I wasn't thinking. The thing broke—worst time of the year for it." He turned and looked at the bull, which was still down on the front end and making spittle sounds. "I hope I didn't kill him. He's a good bull."

Clair turned to Louie. I had never seen her say anything about work to anybody except for when she talked to the cows when we were milking, but she had a hard part in her voice now that made it clear things would happen just as she said.

"Find me some boards and cord to make a splint. Right away. Then you start the truck. We've got to fetch Knute to the doctor in Pinewood to straighten his arm. I'll be driving. You stay here and get chores done and we'll be back tonight." She turned to me. "You're going to have to help Glennis until Harris can work . . ."

I nodded. The look on Harris's face—which I suspected wasn't real—indicated that he probably wouldn't be able to work for a while.

Louie came with some pieces of lath, which he broke in two-foot lengths, and he and Clair made a splint around the break and tied it with cord. Knute stood quietly all the while, watching them with interest but no sign of pain or discomfort, and I truly think he was more concerned about the bull than he was about his arm.

As soon as the splint was on, Louie started the truck, Knute got in one side and Clair the other, and they drove off, the four of us watching them leave.

We were not to see them for two days and I thought by the end of the first day I would die.

When Clair said help Glennis I had no idea how much work it would involve.

Glennis and Louie milked and I had to run back and forth with the full buckets, pour them into the separator, turn the separator, and then when milking was done, clean the barn with a shovel that slid down the gutters to scoop them out.

Then I'd cool all the milk and cream, feed the chickens, move the cows back out of the barn into the pasture, then up to the house to peel potatoes for Glennis to cook, and wash separator parts while she was cooking, and finally sit at the table in the light from the Coleman, trying to stay awake until Louie was done feeding so I could get some.

And all the while Harris was near me, holding

his ribs and stomach, wincing dramatically, instructing me.

"This way, scoop the stuff *this* way" and "You've got to spread the chicken feed out, you dope, or they don't all get some."

By dark I couldn't see and pretty much wished Harris had been killed by the bull, which had gotten up just after Clair and Knute left and seemed none the worse for wear.

On the second day it was harder. We just went at it all day, one job feeding into the next without a break until dark, and Harris still didn't help, which by this time had me furious.

We were in bed. Or rather Harris was in bed and I was about to fall on mine and go into a work-induced coma.

Harris moaned. "I think my ribs are broken."

I said nothing, lay with my eyes closed.

"That bull hit me hard."

Nothing. For a long time, silence. I was in agony, my muscles on fire. Every bone in my body ached.

"In fact I'm thinking I might not be able to do anything for a week or so, what with rib breaks and all . . ."

"Harris," I interrupted.

"What?"

"If you don't help tomorrow, I'm going to kill you." I was surprised to find that I meant it. Completely. And it must have shown in my voice because after a long pause Harris sighed.

"It must have been the way I was lying. I turned a little and the pain is gone."

"Good."

10

*In which I discover love only to have
my heart broken and in revenge
I fry Harris's business*

I didn't know I was in love until it was all over and it was too late to do anything about it.

Knute came home with a plaster cast on his lower left arm and everything went back to normal. He worked as hard as ever and the only change seemed to be that he held his morning coffee with one hand instead of two.

Love started at the Saturday night dance. Somebody else had burned out or was sick or had run out of money or something—it was never exactly clear to me what had happened, and there was always something happening that required Saturday night dances—and we went to town as we usually did.

I had done this several times now and knew what

to expect. I still didn't fit in very well, didn't know any of the other kids, so as soon as I got inside the beer hall, while Harris was fighting—and he fought every single time we went to the Saturday night dance—I got an orange pop and sat at a table in the corner until the movie started.

Usually nobody bothered me. When Harris was done fighting he would come inside and get a pop and sit with me and then we'd go in and watch Gene ride and shoot. Or Harris would—he never tired of Gene riding and shooting. I soon grew bored with it all and on this particular night I was leaning back a bit on my beer crate not looking at the screen but at the faces of the other kids in the room.

There were fourteen or fifteen of them, ranging in age from six to thirteen or so. As soon as hard puberty hit they would be out dancing or in the front of the saloon necking, and the cutoff seemed to be twelve or thirteen.

I couldn't believe they never got sick of the movie and I was watching them watch when I felt somebody doing the same thing to me and turned to see the most beautiful girl in the world looking right at me.

She had wide blue eyes and blond hair in braids that hung down her back, and she smiled and didn't look away when I looked at her and I thought I would die.

It was that sudden. I had seen movies where they talked about love at first sight, movies my mother made me sit through, and I was certain that's what was happening here.

I turned away, could feel myself blushing savagely, and wished I could just crawl away. I decided in fact to do just that and made my way to the door and out into the dance room where the music was whanging and whooshing away.

It was probably all a mistake. She hadn't really been looking at me, I thought, and took an orange pop and went to my little corner table to watch the dancers.

But when I turned to sit I saw that she had followed me and she sat at the same table.

"Hi. I'm Elaine."

I couldn't say anything. She was about my age and when I saw her closely in the better light from the ceiling Coleman lanterns she looked even more beautiful. Her eyes seemed to be made of cool ice and she was wearing a blue dress that matched the color perfectly.

"Elaine Peterson."

Still I sat silent. Shyness, always a problem with me, now became a terminal illness. I thought I would burst, that in some way the shyness would stop my heart. I could hear it beating, whumping, and the beat seemed irregular and it seemed entirely possible that

I would just sit there, like a turd, and die. I took a breath, held it, controlled my voice as much as possible, and blurted my name.

She smiled. "We live near Greener Lake—about four miles from the Larsons."

I asked her why I hadn't seen her at the movie—or thought I did. It came out: 'Haven'tseenmovieyou?" Or something near it.

"I've been staying with my grandmother in North Dakota. It's over west of here a hundred and fifty miles."

She said it like it was another country and I thought I might tell her that I had lived in the Philippines for almost three years and in Texas and had seen California and pretty much everything in between but nothing, absolutely nothing came out.

I don't know how long we could have gone on like that, her talking, me with my tongue clove to the roof of my mouth, wishing I could disappear, but time kicked in and took over. It was late and the band started on its last dance, a slow waltz, and the movie was done and the rest of the kids came out of the back room.

Harris spied me instantly and took in the situation in a glance. He came up to the table—the ubiquitous bottle of orange pop in his hand—and plunked down in a chair.

I made eye motions at him to leave but he ignored them and spoke to Elaine.

"How do you like my cousin?"

She smiled. "He seems nice."

Harris shook his head. "That's what I thought but he ain't right."

I pushed at his shoulder.

"What do you mean?" she asked.

"In the head. He ain't right. It was something to do with when he was borned. They cut the cord too fast or something and his brain didn't get into the light. It happens all the time. Brains got to get into the light or they don't work right. You remember that Severson kid? How he kept leaning left and ate his snot all the time?" Harris pointed at me with his chin. "It's the same with him."

"Not true . . . ," I said, or attempted to—it really came out as more of a *blapp*. The shyness had gotten worse and I was now in the position of having to convince Elaine that I was indeed "right in the head " and did not eat my snot, without being able to speak but it was too late. Elaine was studying me with a new look, one of pity, and she smiled—not unkindly—and nodded and left me sitting there with Harris, fuming.

"I'll get you for this," I told him.

"Ahh you didn't want to mess around with Elaine anyway. Pretty soon you'd just want to go down there all the time and then I'd have nobody to play with and there you'd be, hanging around their mailbox hoping to see her . . ."

"I'll get you for this," I repeated. "I really will."

And as luck would have it I got my chance the very next day.

"I ain't gonna do it."

Harris stood by the side of the barn, looking at the wire that came from an insulator near the door and led out into the pasture.

Knute had turned the pigs out into a part of the cow pasture to root and dig for a while. Rather than put up hog fence he bought a battery-operated electric fencer and some insulators and wire.

Inside the barn he put a dry-cell, six-volt battery and the fencer to keep them out of the weather, then brought the wire out through a hole.

We had half a good day watching the sows figure the wire out. They learned fast and one of them, old Gertie, learned on the first day to cake mud on her head, let it dry, and then push at the wire with the dry mud insulator to get out of the pasture and into the cornfield.

The chickens hit it a few times, squawking and jumping with feathers flying, and even Buzzer accidentally brushed the wire. When it popped him he took it as an attack and went after it, which of course made it worse and made him more angry so that he attacked harder, biting and clawing at the wire until finally he admitted defeat and walked away from the fence. Every hair on his body was straight out and I believe if anybody had crossed him right then he would have killed.

It was while Buzzer was fighting the wire that the idea came. We had tried touching it with the backs of our fingers and pieces of grass but the results were inconclusive. I had always been of a scientific nature, believed in the worth of experiments, and I wondered what would happen—watching Buzzer and the fence at war—if somebody actually peed on the wire.

Specifically I wondered what would happen if *Harris* peed on the wire.

I knew it would not be an easy experiment to conduct and set about doing it carefully. The subject would be reluctant—downright negative, as it turned out—and there would have to be some form of inducement so attractive that it would overcome the reluctance.

As it happened I had the "dourty peectures."

The power of these pictures to control and induce were beyond question. I believe if given enough of them Harris would have walked into a bonfire—indeed, I would have done the same thing. The quality of the pictures wasn't great. They were black-and-white and small and grainy. But they worked. It was impossible to look at them and still breathe correctly. My dilemma was mostly one of quantity. I knew I could get the experiment to work, but with how much effort?

How many pictures would it take?

I had, altogether, seven of them and since I was interested in them myself—purely from an artistic viewpoint, of course—I didn't want to completely deplete the collection.

I offered Harris one picture. It was not the best picture—the best picture I wouldn't have released if Harris had bitten the wire and hung on with his mouth (something I considered suggesting when I remembered what he had done with the first love of my life)—but it was a good picture: accurate in detail, fundamentally sound as far as composition and educational benefits were concerned, and far reaching in its ability to promote advanced stages of hyperventilation.

"Nope," he repeated. "I ain't gonna do it."

But his refusal was soft. I could sense the weakness in it and I countered. The picture I'd offered, plus one other, the one where it was possible to See It All.

"Well . . ."

I had him.

"First the rules."

"What rules?"

"You have to pee right on the wire—not just pass over it—and you have to pee on it long enough to get the surge." (It was a pulse fencer, not on continuously but pulsing at one-second intervals.) "Otherwise it's not a deal."

He thought another minute, studying the wire. "That thing put a sow on her knees . . ."

I shook my head. "She was off balance. Besides, two of the pictures for your very own—that's a good swap."

Yet another minute, then a sigh. "All right. Go get the pictures."

I ran to the house, took out the two selected pictures, put them under my shirt, and trotted back to the barn where Harris was still standing, looking at the wire.

"I've got them."

"Let me see."

I raised my shirt and showed him the pictures, lowered it. "So go ahead—pee on it."

He unbuttoned the fly on his bibs and took his business out, then stood there, frowning.

"What's the matter?"

"It don't work. Nothing's coming out."

"Push a little."

"I am. It's scared. It don't want to do it."

"If you don't pee on the wire, the deal is off," I reminded him, thinking it would prompt action.

"I know, I know. It just won't work." His frown deepened. "It's like it knows what's coming and don't want to do it."

"Two pictures . . ."

"I'll have to lie to it."

"Lie to what?"

"My business. I'll just have to lie to it and start peeing over here, then swing it around, make the dumb thing think everything is all right."

He turned sideways, aimed away from the fence, and in a moment it started.

"So turn," I said. "Before it's done."

"It ain't that easy. Something in me won't let it happen . . ."

"Ahh heck, you're going to run out."

"No, I'm holding her back. Here, now . . ."

He turned slowly until the stream of urine was only inches away from the wire, hung there for a second, then hit the wire.

"There," he said, "now are you hap—"

He had crossed the wire between pulses, when the electricity wasn't moving through the wire, and the pulse hit him halfway through the word *happy*.

Later I would come to know a great deal about electrical things. I would understand that water is an excellent conductor of electrical energy but that urine, with its higher mineral content, is even better and what Harris did amounted to hooking a copper wire from his business to the electric fence.

The results were immediate, and everything I would have hoped for from a standpoint of scientific observation, not to mention revenge.

In a massive galvanic reaction every muscle in Harris's body convulsively contracted, jerking like a giant spring had tightened inside him.

He went stiff as a poker, then soared up and over backward in a complete flip, arcing a stream that caught the afternoon sun so I swore I could see a rainbow in it.

Nor did the spectacle end when he hit the ground. He landed on his side, both legs pumping, then sprung to his feet, running in tight circles holding himself and hissing:

"Oh-God-oh-God-oh-God-oh . . ."

All in all it was well worth the investment and when he finally settled, leaning against the barn wall holding his business, panting loudly, I reached under my shirt to give him the two pictures.

It was not to be, and the exact responsibility of who owed whom pictures would plague us the rest of the summer and perhaps does yet.

As I held the pictures toward Harris and he released his groin long enough to reach for them a shadow fell over us and I turned to see Louie standing there.

He reached down with a crooked, filthy hand and took the pictures, held them up to the light, smiled toothlessly, and walked away toward the granary, putting the pictures in the top pocket of his bibs.

"Damn." Harris spoke quietly and his voice was shaking. "You owe me two pictures."

"It wasn't my fault. I held them out to you. Louie took them."

"They wasn't halfway." He hissed like a snake. "They wasn't even close to halfway."

"They were over halfway."

"You *liar*."

"I'm not lying. I handed the pictures over to you and you were reaching for them when Louie grabbed them. I did what I was supposed to do."

"*You* did?" He sneered, or grimaced in pain, it was hard to tell the difference. "*I* peed on the wire . . ."

Later that night, lying in bed in the darkened room, listening to the drone of mosquitoes fighting the screen, I remembered him hitting the wire and started laughing.

"It ain't funny," he said from the other bed. "I'm all swoll up. It's like my business was hit by lightning."

"It is too funny. You ran in little circles yelling,

'Oh-God-oh-God-oh-God . . .' " I had to bury my face in the pillow to hold the sound of laughing down so it wouldn't wake the grown-ups.

For a time there was silence, then he giggled. "I think I saw him."

"Who?"

"Jesus, you dope. But he wasn't in no peach tree . . ."

And still later, when the giggling had subsided and we were nearly asleep, through a half doze I heard him one more time:

"You still owe me two pictures."

"No, I don't."

"You do."

"Don't."

"Do."

11

In which Harris discovers speed . . .
and the value of clothing

Here's the problem—it's too slow. Hell, we can ride Bob and Bill and go faster."

I could have pointed out that since the loft and shotgun incidents there had been absolutely no way we could get close enough to Bob or Bill to touch them, let alone ride them. But it had not been long since lightning had hit Harris's business, so arguing with him about things seemed too harsh; Harris still walked with his legs apart a bit.

Besides, I agreed with him.

We had pulled two old bicycles from the junk heap and worked almost three days loosening the chains, oiling them, fixing tubes and pumping tires, twisting and aligning handlebars, and greasing bearings—all just to ride up and back on the quarter-mile drive-way.

Initially I had in mind a fantasy involving getting a bike fixed and then pedaling the four miles to Elaine's farm. I had seen her once since the night she'd learned about my brain being late getting into the light, at another Saturday night dance. And while I apparently still loved her with all my heart—or so it felt, judging by my breathing and pulse—she only smiled, again not unkindly, but otherwise ignored me completely.

Love is persistent, however, at least in the imagination, and my brain—light enfeebled as it may have been—would not stop thinking of her golden hair, blue eyes, even smile, and soft voice.

So the fantasies ran. I would fix a bike, I would pedal to her farm—though I had no idea where it was—and coming out to the mailbox she would see me pedaling by and stop and talk to me and find out that my brain was all right and smile at me the other way and we would kiss and we would marry and we would . . .

All this until we actually got the bikes working and pedaled the length of the driveway and back, grinding along, the wheels so out of line they wobbled, the tires bulging at the sides. After one loop I thought less of love and more of the possible terminal effects of trying to pedal four miles, and that had brought us to Harris's trenchant remark, which he now repeated.

"Too slow. We need something to get these gooners moving. We need some kind of motor . . ." He stood with his hands in the pockets of his bibs, studying the yard, and I think had actually scanned it twice when he saw the washing machine.

His eyes stopped moving and I saw him start chewing his bottom lip. It was a habit I'd come to know as an indication that we would soon be in trouble—or more trouble than normal—but one that I also had come to view with some excitement.

The washing machine was by the house. There was no electricity yet in that country and some families still used hand washboards. But Knute and Clair had some years earlier purchased an old gas-engine washer.

It looked like a regular wringer washer except that underneath it had a one-cylinder gas motor with a tiny gas tank and a foot kick-starter that stuck out to the side.

I had seen Clair and Glennis use the washer. It ran with a *put-n-put-n-put* that became a one-speed drone, controlled by a governor that cranked the washer and wringer assembly with a V-belt off a pulley on the motor.

Harris wandered near the washer and studied it more closely, keeping well clear of the kitchen window where Clair and Glennis were working.

"She'll do her," he said, nodding.

"Do what?"

"Pull that bicycle."

"The washing machine?"

"The motor, you dope. It's only held on there by four bolts. We'll take her off and bolt her on a bike and rig up a belt and off we go."

Off you *go*, I thought, remembering the horse and shotgun, but I said nothing about it. I was also thinking of one salient fact that perhaps Harris had overlooked.

"The motor," I pointed out in a slightly superior air, "is attached to your mother's washing machine."

"*I* know that," he said, looking at me as if I'd gone insane. "We'll just have to wait until they go to town."

It was then that I realized the complexity of Harris's plans. He didn't just do things as they came along, willy-nilly—often he schemed for days, worked on them. Like the time he tried to shoot a banty chicken out of an old stovepipe with compressed air. It took hours of hand-pumping air into an inner tube inside a stovepipe until it was ready to burst, then getting the pipe situated and catching a chicken and jamming her down into the stovepipe (I suggested Ernie but we couldn't find him). And even when the results didn't warrant the effort—he had feathers blown two inches into his nostrils when the stovepipe burst—he was optimistic about the outcome. ("Fastest *that* chicken ever flew—she had to be doing two hundred when she hit my face.")

And the plan he set into effect now was such a long-term effort.

From an old swatting machine he found a V-belt pulley wheel about a foot and a half across and used a hacksaw to cut the four center spokes out of it, leaving a four-inch piece on each spoke.

He then pulled the back wheel off the better of the two bicycles and spent hours wiring and friction-taping the pulley to the spokes.

By this time I was bored and looking for other things to do. I sneaked up into the granary, as I often did, and looked at Louie's diorama and was surprised to find that he had added to it.

There was a new farm, with little trees and a house, and with a start I realized it was our farm. He'd done a model of the Larson place: a miniature copy of the house made of paper and cardboard with trees around it and a model of the barn. There were figures for Clair and Glennis—the two of them standing by the house—and one of Knute working on a small team of horses and another for Louie himself upright near the head of the team. And there were two more figures, near the hog pen, playing in the dirt.

Harris and me.

There was a figure for me.

A strange feeling came over me, seeing the figure. I somehow had never belonged—always felt like a visitor. And though we were related I never thought of myself as part of the family in some way; I considered myself more an observer than an outsider, a friend who watches.

The figure made my role different, carved it in time. I wasn't just a visiting second cousin. I was somebody, a part of this place, this family. I belonged.

I picked up the figure that represented me and looked more closely at it. It was wearing a mouse-hair coat and had a smile and white teeth inside the little smile. It couldn't have looked less like me but at the same time made me think more of myself, my life, than anything ever had before and I was crying when I set it down, crying to myself thinking that I felt like I was home.

"What's wrong?" Harris was working on the bicycle when I came back down and he saw my red eyes.

"Dust. I was up in the granary."

"Did you find 'em?"

"What . . . Oh, no." Harris was still suffering from

the purloined pictures and his sore business and believed that Louie had hidden the pictures somewhere in the granary. Harris felt he had proprietary rights and was hoping to find the pictures and steal them back. "I didn't see them."

"He's probably got 'em under something. Did you look under things?"

"No . . ."

"Well, it don't matter. Here, look at this—ain't this a beauty?"

He pointed to the bike with the pulley wired/taped onto the rear wheel. He had reaffixed the wheel to the rear and held it up to spin it to show that it rotated freely.

I nodded dubiously. It seemed more like a rotating bandage than anything else, and I couldn't see how it would possibly work, but I didn't have Harris's enthusiasm and optimism, couldn't see the big picture as well as he did.

He had also manufactured a crude wooden platform, which was bolted above the pedals and rusty chain guard with two U-bolts.

"For the motor."

I nodded again but in truth I didn't think there would ever be a chance to try it. Knute and the rest didn't go to town that often. Usually somebody stayed home. But I was wrong again. The next day Knute fired up the truck and took Clair and Glennis to town and Louie took the team six miles to a neighbor's to get the horses shod.

Harris watched the grain wagon trundling off down the driveway with Louie sitting up in the high seat.

He had a crescent wrench hidden behind his back and as soon as Louie was well clear of the house he went for the washing machine.

I grabbed his suspenders and stopped him. "Just so you know—I'm not taking the blame this time."

"They won't even know we done it."

"*You've* done it."

"Yeah. They won't even know. We'll hook her in and make a few runs and put the motor back on the washing machine."

"Just the same. No matter what, I'm not taking the blame."

He nodded. "Sure. But you'll see, there won't be no problem . . ."

Of all the understatements Harris made that summer, it was perhaps the greatest.

At no time during the ensuing disaster did I think the contraption would really work. I helped him unbolt the four bolts that held the motor to the washing machine and helped him carry it to the bike and put it on the platform.

He had an old auger bit-and-brace and a long V-belt from the granary, one of the spares for the binder. It took him just a few minutes to remove the back wheel of the bike and loop the belt through and put the wheel back on, fit the belt into the taped pulley, and then connect it to the drive pulley on the motor.

He adjusted the motor into position, marked the holes, and then augered four holes through the wooden platform and bolted the motor in place with the belt tight.

"There," he said. "She ought to fly."

Or blow up, I thought. "How are you going to start it?" The kick starter was up against the frame.

"I'll push the bike until she fires, then jump on. You be running in back of me and climb on when I get on."

"I'm not riding that thing."

He studied me. "You chicken."

"I'm still not riding it."

He frowned. "All right. We need a timer so's we can check our speed. You run get the alarm clock from the folks' bedroom."

I did as he told me. It was a brass clock with two bells on top and a hammer that went back and forth to ring them.

"Take the other bike to the end of the driveway and when I start the engine and you hear me let her rip, you check the clock and then when I get to the end of the driveway you check her again and we'll be able to figure out how fast I went."

I was skeptical. My personal feelings were that

he would never get the contraption out of the yard, let alone to the end of the driveway. But Harris had surprised me before—almost continuously—and so I took the other bike and dutifully pedaled to the end of the driveway and waited.

And waited.

I checked the clock numerous times as I heard Harris trying to start the motor back in the yard.

Put-n-put-n-put . . .

And it would die. I found later that the motor died because Harris had already unhooked the governor and it was getting too much gas and was choking out. I also decided still later that it was probably God trying to save Harris from himself. But even divine intervention didn't work, and in truth Harris was so determined probably nothing could have saved him. Or, as Harris put it later, speaking of God: "At *least* He could have stopped me from unhooking that stupid governor . . ."

The motor started, finally, with a stuttering *put-n-put-n-put* and as soon as I saw Harris begin to move I looked down at the clock. I couldn't have had my eyes down for more than three seconds, but when I brought them up I was surprised to see that Harris had already moved toward me some distance.

Several other things were happening by this time that would determine Harris's fate. The engine, starved of gasoline all its life on the washing machine by the mechanical governor, responded in explosive gratitude for the chance at freedom. It went from the subdued *put-n-put-n-put* to a healthy *BAM-BAM-BAM* that I could hear easily from the end of the driveway.

Then, too, there was the further bad luck that somehow, in some way, everything held together. Bolts, belts, the bicycle—everything miraculously stayed in one piece and all of the gasoline that poured into the wide open throat of the little Briggs and Stratton engine was translated into power at the back wheel.

Power and speed.

From that point on everything came in flashes, flickering scenes of disaster, like watching a stop-action film of a flood or a hurricane hitting the coast of Florida.

To give him his due, Harris was plucky. Early on the Bendix brake had jammed and the chain—and therefore pedals—had turned with the back wheel. Harris kept his feet on the pedals, or tried to, but as the speed went up and the pedals began to turn faster, much faster than they'd ever turned, his legs became at first a blur, then he held them up, the pedals slapping the bottoms of his bare feet as the bike approached something like terminal velocity with Harris just along for the ride.

It was amazing that nothing fell apart. As he got

closer, his knees up alongside his cheeks, I could see that sense had at last come into his mind and his eyes were wide, *huge* with fear. His tongue hung out the side of his mouth, spit flying, and he turned into a blur.

Fifteen, twenty, thirty, forty—the bike had to be doing close to fifty miles an hour when he passed me standing at the end of the driveway.

"Helpppp meeeeee!" he yelled, the Doppler effect changing the pitch of his plea as he cleared the end of the driveway, flew across in front of me, and hit the ditch on the far side of the county road like a meteorite.

It was then, as he put it later, that he realized he was in trouble. Making the turn onto the road was clearly impossible but he claims he still thought he could "slow her down in the brush along the ditch."

The brush slowed him, all right. It stopped the bike dead in a dazzling, cartwheeling spray of engine, spokes, wheels, frame, and tangled belt. For half a second it was impossible to tell where Harris ended and bicycle began; the whole seemed a jumbled mass of boy and machine.

Then Harris separated. His body high above the brush, spread-eagled—he claimed later he could see for miles—still moving close to fifty miles an hour, then fell down, down in a curving arc to hit the ground and explode in a flurry of willows, leaves, brush, and dirt.

Then silence, broken only by the soft hissing of gas running from the tank onto the engine and the ticking of the brass alarm clock.

"Harris?"

Nothing.

"Harris—are you all right?"

A spitting sound—leaves and dirt being expelled. Then a grunt. "Hell no, I ain't all right. I was stuck in the dirt like an arrow and I'm all over scratches."

"Do you need help?" I couldn't see him for the brush and willows.

"Yeah. Help me find my bibs."

"Your pants?"

"Yeah—they come off me somewhere."

We looked for half an hour and more, Harris hiding twice when cars went by on the road, and we didn't find them and we looked for another half hour and we still didn't find them and we never did.

We finally gave up. The bike was a total loss but the engine was cast iron and undamaged and we put it on the seat of my bike and held it there while we wheeled it back to the yard and the washing machine, Harris walking alongside naked as a bird and all over scratches as he'd said.

Later that night we were lying in our beds in the

dark, nightbirds singing outside the window, and Harris whispered, "How fast was I going?"

I shook my head, then realized he couldn't see me in the dark. "I don't know."

"What did the clock say?"

"I forgot to look at it."

"You *forgot?*"

"I'm sorry."

"I go through this and have to tell Pa I lost my pants somewhere and you forgot to look at the clock?"

"I said I'm sorry."

There was a long quiet. "How fast do you *think* I was going?"

I thought long before answering, remembered his eyes, his legs pumping, the motor pounding as he went by, the crash in the brushy ditch, the sight of him flying through the air, losing his pants.

"At least a hundred."

Another soft silence, then a sigh. "I thought so— the fence posts looked like chicken netting. It was really something."

"Yes. It was really something . . ."

12

In which all things change

The time of summer ended suddenly enough.
In the fields along the driveway there was
a forty-acre piece in corn. It was silage, or
field corn—as opposed to sweet corn—and meant to
feed the milk cows in the winter and grew to truly
gigantic proportions.

Plants seven feet tall were not uncommon and
from our perspective—between four and five feet—
as the stalks grew taller the field became an inviting
green jungle. By lying on the ground it was possible
to see down the rows through a cleared area about a
foot high, before the leaves started. But standing lim-
ited visibility to a few feet in any direction and the
field became a perfect place to play hide-and-seek.

Or ambush.

Or, as Harris put it, "It's time for cob wars."

The corn ears weren't fully ripe and wouldn't be until later in the summer, or early fall, when they would be chopped for silage and stored in a silage pit. But they had developed enough to make almost perfect missiles of nearly a pound and when thrown correctly, with a flick of the wrist, if they hit you in the head they'd put you down.

"It's this way," Harris explained to me. "You go in the corn first and be the commie jap and I'll give you a head start and then come after you."

"Who are you?"

"I'm GI Joe."

"Why do I have to be the commie jap? I want to be GI Joe."

Harris studied me and sighed. "Look, who made the game up—me or you?"

"Well, you . . ."

"And who knows the rules?"

"I didn't know there *were* any rules . . ."

"Me, that's who. So I have to be the one to hang back and make sure it's all working right and that makes *you* the commie jap and me GI Joe. It just figures."

It didn't actually figure that way to me but it was clear that if we were going to play I would have to be the commie jap, and so I at length nodded and moved into the corn.

It was like stepping into another world. Light filtered down through the plants and cast a green glow that made me want to walk softly and whisper, and I crouched and moved forward carefully.

I hadn't gone eight feet when something hit me in the back of the head so hard my eyes crossed.

"Got you, you gooner commie jap!"

I wheeled and there was nothing. Just the rustling green corn. I took two steps, started the third, and took another cob in the back of the head.

"Dammit, Harris—quit that!"

". . . commie jap gooner . . ."

And he was gone again. But this time I heard him and thinking I was about to be hit again dropped to my stomach and found the clear area.

There he was, or his legs. Two rows over and slightly toward the road. I smiled, pulled an ear of corn off the nearest plant, slithered on my belly two rows over, rose suddenly, and threw the cob as hard as I could where he had been standing.

And missed.

"Fell for it, you commie jap gooner!"

And another cob caught me in the back of the head. Somehow as I rose he had dropped and gone around in back of me for a rear attack. This time the cob caught me hard enough to make my ears ring, and rage took over any thought and I went for him.

From that point on it disintegrated into a catch-me-if-you-can brawl with me chasing him through the corn until I couldn't run and both of us, finally, falling to the ground, laughing inside the corn near the edge of the driveway.

"You make a miserable commie jap," Harris said, lying back in the dirt.

"That's because I was supposed to be GI Joe . . ."

The sound of a car engine stopped me and we peeped out of the corn just in time to see the deputy's car go by, headed for the house.

"It's the same guy who brought me," I said. "I wonder what he wants?"

"You, likely. He's come to take you home . . ."

I knew instantly that Harris was right, that the summer was done, and everything in me rebelled. I had come to belong here, wanted to be here, thought of this as home, Harris as a brother and Glennis as a sister and Knute as a pa and Clair as a mother, and didn't, didn't ever want to leave.

"You don't got to go." Harris had read my expression. "You can stay here in the corn. I'll bring you food and a blanket and they'll never find you in a hundred years." His face had a worried, almost frightened look to it and he seemed on the edge of tears.

It was all too sudden. A part of me nodded, wanted to do it, hide, hide, but I knew it wouldn't work. I could hear Clair calling from the house now, calling my name and Harris's name, and fighting it every inch of the way I stood and walked out of the corn and back to the house while Harris stayed in the corn.

Glennis had my box from the room waiting by the deputy's car and she smiled and handed it to me.

"Isn't this nice?" Clair said. "You're going home at last . . ."

But she didn't look happy about it and neither did Knute, who came from near the granary, walking with his hands in his bib pockets, balled into fists, looking at the ground. Louie was nowhere to be seen.

Knute said nothing but stood next to Clair and Glennis was crying silently and I got in the car, all in moments, and the deputy turned around and we went down the driveway and away from the farm. Or tried to. We hadn't gone a hundred yards when I saw Harris come boiling out of the corn, his bibs all over mud and his hands waving to stop the car.

He came to my side and I rolled the window down.

"You don't got to stay gone, you know," he said, and he was crying so naturally I started to cry too. "You can talk to them gooners and tell them you got to come back here."

"I will."

"You make them bring you back."

"I will."

And the deputy pulled away and we left Harris standing there by the side of the driveway. I looked back out the rear window and he was waving one hand so I waved back but soon he was lost from view and the rest of the farm was gone and we were on the road heading back to town.

The deputy spat out the window. "Nice people, the Larsons. You have a good summer?"

And it was all there. The horses and the pigs and Ernie and the pictures and Louie and swimming and going to see the Gene Autry movie—all there at once, filling me so that I had to look out the window and hide my eyes.

"Yes. I did. I had a nice summer."

EPILOGUE

Three weeks after I had returned home I received a small package with the following letter inside:

Dear Gooner:

You know I don't write so good so Glennis is doing this for me except I'm worried she won't say what I want and I don't trust the big . . .

There, right there she hit me. I didn't say nothing wrong and she whacked me, so you can see things ain't changed a whole lot.

I thought I'd killed Ernie when I ran over him with a wheelbarrow full of sand when he wasn't looking but I didn't. Kill him, I mean. The son . . . There, she hit me again. Ernie laid there for a minute and then got up and made it under the granary before I could get the wheelbarrow turned around for another run on him. I would have turned faster except I wetted the sand down to make it good and heavy and the extra weight slowed me some.

Everybody else is fine. Pa broke a finger but it don't seem to bother him none. Ma is cooking. Glennis is looking all moon-eyed at Clyde Peterson . . . There, she hit me again. But she is. He's took to hanging around smelling at the gatepost . . . I wish she'd stop that. I keep getting whacked and don't even mean it.

Buzzer is all right although he seems cross sometimes and popped me once last week.

I found some graves back down off the house from homesteaders and was thinking I'd dig them up and look for treasure but I'll wait until you come back for that.

Well, that's all for now. Oh, Louie come in the other day and told me to mail you what's in the package. He said you'd know what it was.

Bye, you old gooner, and I hope you can come home soon.

Harris

I unwrapped a piece of paper in the box and found the small figure that had been me in Louie's diorama. I held the mouse-furred little statue for a long time, rolling it in my fingers, then I put it on a windowsill where I could see it while I drifted to sleep that night and dreamed of horses and farms and corn and girls with blond hair and Tarzan and Gene and a bicycle that did a hundred miles an hour, carrying a freckled boy in bibs . . .